THE KEY

J.D. BUCHMILLER

Published 2021 by Your Book Angel

The characters are all mine, any similarities with other fictional or real persons/places are coincidental.

Printed in the United States
Edited by Keidi Keating
Layout by Rochelle Mensidor

ISBN:

DEDICATION

Dedicated to my Grandmother, Bonnie Lee Teeter

July 4th, 1947 - February 3rd, 2012

I love and miss you. Rest in peace.

ACKNOWLEDGEMENTS

A thanks to Jeffrey Michael Benjamin for the idea of an underground army. I couldn't have completed this book without you.

Prologue

Three hundred years had passed and there were new rulers to the kingdoms on land and the empire under the sea. Gerardo had left his mark on the hearts of the seapeople and his name had gone down into history on land and throughout the five oceans. Gerardo's only child, a son he and Mira named Jaskaran, became emperor after he married a naiad named Renée. Renée was infertile, so she and Jaskaran adopted a mermaid and named her Nadia. After a ceremony to make her heir, Nadia became the only heir to the throne. It was not long after that Nadia became deathly ill and Renée refused to leave her child's bedside. A couple more months passed, and the miracle worker whom the emperor and empress hired said that Nadia was getting better and should be healthy again in a year, but when Renée looked at her daughter, she didn't believe the miracle worker and remained hopeless.

Month after month, Renée watched over her daughter waiting for her to show signs of healing, and as each day passed and Renée saw nothing changing in her child's face, she became more and more depressed, worried, and faithless. All possible negative emotions drowned her heart. The sounds of her constant wailing, her curses toward random people, and her obnoxious crying could be heard all over the palace and never ceased. After a year, the miracle worker returned to check up on Nadia.

"I find myself baffled, Your Majesties," he said. "She was making so much progress last I saw her. Now, I am sorry to say, it is hopeless. I estimate she has four years to live."

Every day since, the empress spent her time in Nadia's chamber crying. Nothing could make her happy and the more the merfolk tried to lift her spirits, the worse her mood became. Horrible thoughts possessed Renée's mind and she dwelled on them. After several months of extreme mourning, the empress herself became ill, which only worsened her mood.

The sorrow spread with the news throughout all the underwater kingdoms. The oceans were calm and the skies above the water became empty of life and weather. The world wondered why the seas were so quiet and the air so still. The naiads communicated with the forest inhabitants who communicated with those outside the forest. Then, in a little over a week, news about the mood of the empress of the five oceans and the condition of her child had spread throughout all the forest creatures and the sorrow followed with it.

When Jaskaran and the miracle worker walked in to find Nadia's chamber trashed and Renée on the floor weeping and bleeding, the miracle worker banished her to bed away from Nadia for the sake of Nadia's health.

"You cannot take me away from my baby!" she wailed. "I'll have you all beheaded! She's my baby and she's dying! You cannot take me from her!"

She thrashed at everyone who forced her into her bedchamber. She even tried to kill herself. That was when Jaskaran had her tied down.

"Will this end, Miracle Worker?" Jaskaran asked.

"I'm not sure, Your Majesty," the miracle worker answered. "I've seen this go away, and I've seen it last until death."

"With your experience and knowledge, can you make a guess?"

"I'll be honest, Your Majesty. Her condition can possibly last from ten years after Nadia's death to the rest of her life. She seems to have an extremely bad case of depression."

One day during Nadia's tenth year, when Emperor Jaskaran had the time, he came in and sat on the sponge mattress of their clamshell bed next to his wife. He reached over and gently stroked Renée's cheek, waking her. She blinked a couple times and looked up at her husband.

"You shouldn't be so upset, Renée," Jaskaran said.

"Our baby is dying, Jaskaran!" Renée replied. "Why don't you care?"

"I do care, Renée." There was a moment of silence when Renée started crying again. "You need to go see the Miracle Worker at Moss Canyon."

Renée stopped crying and gaped at Jaskaran. "What? The Moss Can—are you mad??"

"She requested to see you, Renée." Jaskaran untied her. "Maybe she can help you. Maybe she can help Nadia."

"I doubt it."

"Renée, go," Jaskaran said sternly.

Then before there was any more arguing, Emperor Jaskaran glided out of the bedchamber and left his wife there with nothing else to do. So, Empress Renée got out of bed and went to the Moss Canyon.

The Moss Canyon was very far away. As Empress Renée traveled further from Coral City where the palace was located, the water grew darker and darker. Even the glowing fish around her didn't offer much help in lighting her way. She almost ran into a thousand sea creatures, rocks, and cliffs, but soon there was a dim, red glow that came from behind a large rock wall some distance ahead. She flowed toward that red glow wondering if she was lost, but to her relief, it was the Moss Canyon. Empress Renée discovered that a lava river created this faint red glow. The river led into a wrecked ship that seemed to have sunk recently. The ship was surrounded by tiny volcanoes that oozed lava into this river. The empress flowed over to the entrance of the ship and stood there, wondering if she should enter.

"Come in, Dear," said a cackling voice from deeper inside the ship. The voice had a strange accent and Empress

Renée winced at the sound of it. "Well come on! I been waiting a long time for you already, don't keep me waiting any longer! We gots tings to talk about!"

Slowly, Empress Renée stepped in and avoided the lava river which seemed to flow straight through to the stern of the ship. The place had been completely remodeled to fit a miracle worker's purposes. Empress Renée wanted to know how the ship didn't rot, mold, or especially burn down being surrounded by lava. Behind a marble podium, was the miracle worker who looked like a hideous hag with an eel's tail. One of her eyes was yellow and the other a fiery orange and they burned through the empress's soul.

"There you are," said the hag with a smile that revealed four missing front teeth. "Follow me and we have foam tea." She turned around to lead the young empress deeper into the ship. "We have much to talk about."

Empress Renée maneuvered around the podium and hesitantly followed the hag.

"Have a seat while I set up the teakettle," the hag offered. The empress obeyed.

"So," Empress Renée said shyly after a long silence. "What was it that you wanted to talk to me about?"

"It's about your daughter, um, oh what's her name?"

"Nadia," the empress reminded.

"Ah, yes!" exclaimed the hag. "That's her name! Anyway, we needs to talk about you and your daughter."

"Me and my daughter?"

"Yes, and we start with you." The hag approached the table with two cups of foam tea. She gave one to the empress. "You're stressed out. Why?"

"My daughter is sick and she won't get better," Empress Renée answered as if it was obvious.

The hag shook her head and Empress Renée looked at her confused. "That's not all. You feel an emptiness inside you also." Empress Renée wondered where the hag was going with this. "Many people do," the hag went on. "But you seem to take it a lot harder than most. You tink your daughter that will fill this emptiness, but you must admit, you were unhappy before your daughter became ill. It will be known, your unhappiness is what made your daughter ill in the first place."

Empress Renée couldn't think of how to respond.

"Did you know that depression is contagious? It spreads troughout the household and eventually leaves the house into the city. Depression makes you more able to get ill! That is what happened to your daughter!"

"So where are you going with this?" asked the empress.

"You want to know what will make your daughter better?" the hag asked taking a sip of her tea.

"Of course!"

"Your daughter was getting better when the miracle worker you hired said she was. Your distrust and negative disposition made her ill again, and she's only getting worse. So it all comes down to this: if you don't become satisfied, if you don't find something to fill your emptiness, your daughter can't stay in the ocean! You kill her! Your daughter is so young, her tiny body can't take the stress like the rest of the world can. You must provide a better, more positive environment for her to live in."

"And how do you expect me to fill this emptiness?" the empress asked in a mocking tone. "Do you even know what this, 'emptiness,' is?"

"You must find out on your own, or there will be no effect," the hag answered. "For instance, I have found God. On my own. Even if you fail to find joy for yourself, you can express joy to others and in turn, provide a more positive environment for your daughter to live in."

"Well, I must say this visit has been fun, and I'm very pleased to hear that my daughter's death will be on me. But I must be going." The empress got up to leave. "Thanks for the tea."

"So this means you don't want to save your daughter's life?"

"Stop pinning it on me!" Empress Renée violently jabbed a finger at the hag.

"You act as if she's already dead. You can easily save her life."

"This is ridiculous." The empress began to walk away again.

"Well then pack her things. She be leaving the ocean tomorrow morning."

"What are you talking about?" Empress Renée asked. "You're not taking her away from me!"

"No, you're abandoning her. And if that won't help you search for happiness, perhaps this will. If you fail, your daughter will also be given this golden ball when she is sent to land." The hag pointed to a golden ball somewhat larger than a baseball. "There, she must keep it hidden. Do you know why?"

"Why?" Empress Renée asked frightened.

"Because it will hold her curse."

"You cursed her?"

"No," the hag answered taking another sip of her tea. "But if you do not become more positive and encouraging of those around you, you will."

Empress Renée was infuriated. "I will have you executed!"

"Take this with you," said the hag ignoring the threat. She handed the empress a key on a gold chain. Engraved in the heart-shaped handle was a rosebud. "Remember the Rose Tree that was planted in honor of your father-in-law?"

"What about it?"

"It's almost finish stretching above the ground. I expect it to be finished growing its leafy branches in about a year or two. Once the rosebud on that key is bloomed, the Rose Tree will have finished growing its branches and your time will be up."

"Time for what?"

"Finding what's missing in your life, of course. To save your daughter's life. Now if all these… warnings, if you will, do not influence you to find something to fill your emptiness, I don't know what will. Too bad your daughter's life isn't enough." The hag began swimming away to clean up the teacups.

"What's that supposed to mean?"

"Notting, notting. Just fill your emptiness before the rose blooms."

"And what if Nadia dies before then?"

"She won't, trust me. I know. She will remain in the same condition she is in at the moment until your time is up. By the way, do not wear that key around your neck. It will hinder your ability to find what's missing in your life."

Renée placed it around her neck. "I'll have you executed." Then she quickly flowed back to the palace to tell her husband everything.

Chapter One

The day was only hitting its peak at the Obsidian Palace where Emperor Jaskaran and his two advisors held a meeting in the grand drawing room. They sat at a round, polished stone table with another naiad and a merman with a shark's tail. The dim light of the glowfish chandelier above them left dramatic shadows on their faces as they feasted on their luncheon and discussed matters light-heartedly. The meeting seemed to be going very well for the emperor and his advisors until a booming voice jolted the smooth current surrounding them.

"I require a word with His Majesty! *Immediately.*"

Jaskaran paused for a moment to eye who had dared interrupted them. When he recognized it was his wife, he breathed a heavy sigh and addressed his guests. "I apologize for this. Please wait outside, we shouldn't be long."

His guests and advisors politely exited the drawing room without a word, but bowed to the empress and left the two alone. Jaskaran endeavored to remain calm as he approached Renée, who stood beside a large desk chipped from stone and painted in gold. They both waited to speak until the door was closed.

"What is it, Renée?" Jaskaran asked.

"I just returned from the miracle worker and she *threatened* me," Renée whined.

"How so?"

"She blamed me for Nadia's illness! She said that if I don't cure my mood within a year, we'll have to send Nadia to shore. *And* she'll be cursed!"

"Then you'd better lighten up, Renée," Jaskaran growled.

Renée gazed at her husband in disappointed shock. "You mean you're not going to do anything about this?"

"What would you have me do, Renée? I've done everything to make you happy, to make you comfortable in my palace! I've allowed you to remain at Nadia's bedside even though everyone advised me not to, and besides that I've done everything in my power to provide Nadia with the best treatment in all the seas!"

Renée was taken aback. "Surely you don't blame me for her illness too!"

"No, I'm to blame as well for letting you poison her with your negativity despite the warnings of numerous miracle workers and advisors!"

"I beg your pardon!"

"Renée, my father believed that there is a noble reason behind everything the miracle worker says and does, thus I trust the same, and you should too. It is apparent to me that you have a mighty task at hand. I urge you to let me know what it is that I can do to aid you for Nadia's good."

"You can have that wretched eel executed and find another miracle worker to heal Nadia!" said Renée as she glared at Jaskaran with her crystal eyes.

"There are no more miracle workers, Renée! This is our last chance! Now did she say anything else I should know about?"

"She said that Nadia's condition will not worsen until my time is up. And she gave me this key." Renée handed the key to Jaskaran. "She said it'll tell me how much time I have left. She also said to keep it hidden, otherwise it'll hinder my ability to find happiness."

"I see you're doing well with that," the emperor deadpanned.

"You know what, Jaskaran," Renée spat. "If you're not going to help then hand me the key and get back to your meeting."

"No, I'm keeping the key so that it remains hidden like the miracle worker directed. Now leave and tell Flint and Maine to return with our guests. I need to complete this meeting."

Renée hesitated for a moment to try and think of something to say to get the key back, but Emperor Jaskaran shot her a look that told her to leave. So she did.

During the many months following her discussion with the miracle worker, Empress Renée roamed around outside the Obsidian Palace in the hope that she could find healing in the empire's ocean-life, but it only reminded her of why she had always locked herself up in the palace to get away from such dirty creatures. She even spent several months visiting her family, but as much as they tried to lift her spirits she wouldn't budge. It only reminded her why she had tried so hard to marry Jaskaran and leave their presence, and thus worsened her mood. Then she spent time in the palace's glowing garden which she had commanded be planted for her to find a median between palace life and ocean-life since neither made her happy. Despite the fact that it was twice the size of the average palace courtyard, it felt much too small for her and was so confining she felt as though she was drowning.

All the while, Renée stewed in the knowledge that everyone blamed her for Nadia's poor health. Hadn't she done everything she could for that child? It wasn't even her child! Why did it seem like everyone cared more about Nadia's health than they cared about their empress's health? How could she make everyone see that she wasn't the villain here? How could she make everyone see that she, too, was a victim? Renée soon grew stressed to the point where she decided that she would have to continue her problem-solving on land, but she needed to take that key with her to know how much time she had left.

One night, about a year and four months after her discussion with the miracle worker, Empress Renée rose from bed while Emperor Jaskaran slept soundly, and she searched her husband's coral drawers for the key. When she didn't find it there, she searched under things, behind things, in boxes and bottles. She couldn't find it anywhere and after a few hours of searching, she opted to give up for the night and went to return to sleep. He must not be keeping it in the bedchamber, so she would have to search elsewhere another time. Perhaps his study.

Then when Renée approached her bed, she noticed a faint gleam beneath her husband's head. She stepped closer and realized that the shiny object was the key itself, hidden beneath Jaskaran's sponge pillow. She almost felt enraged. She knew that this wasn't his original hiding spot for important objects, which only meant that he had been carrying the key on his person this entire time. How could she have not noticed before? Renée breathed deeply in an effort to remain calm. It didn't matter anymore, she had found the key, and it was almost too easy to steal back as more than half of it was visible beneath the pillow. She simply snatched it, wrote a quick note of farewell to her husband, and quickly snuck out of the palace.

Empress Renée made her way alone to the Maja Forest on the continent Noelle where she would often go to consult with Queen Tiana about her troubles. Nearly everyone knew her there, however most were fairly upset with her stubbornly negative disposition and the effects it was having on the world. So, once she surfaced from the Pixie River, no one greeted her.

Renée paid them no attention and ascended the stone steps that led to a grassy cliff overlooking the Pixie Lake. Here, there was a small section of the forest which looked like a polished marble ruin that had been spruced up and decorated. To the left Renée recognized a long ebony table, built and sculpted by none other than the dwarves of the forest. The table was surrounded by thirteen velvet dining chairs, crafted by the same dwarves. A stone statue of a legendary elf stood to the right beneath a silver arch which had been engraved with an Elvic blessing. But what Renée liked most about the area was the solid floor that looked like calm water, which rippled with each of her steps. She found Queen Tiana, a fairy dressed in black, dark green, and dark blue, sitting on her silver throne to the left of this section of forest. Her ashy-gray and silver wings flowed in the soft breeze with her ivory hair as she spoke with a púca, a tiny creature which loved to help people.

"And alert everyone that Avery predicts rain for tomorrow. The sprites and pixies should already be aware, but remind them in case they've forgotten."

"Yes, Your Majesty," the púca replied with a quick, deep bow, and then skipped away to do his queen's bidding.

Here, Queen Tiana glanced up with her bright green eyes and spotted Renée. "Empress Renée! My melancholy friend!" She stood to approach the empress.

"Queen Tiana," Renée replied with a sad smile. "How are you?"

"Very well." They embraced each other. "I suppose there's no need to ask how you're doing."

"I take it you've heard."

"The most recent event I've heard concerning you is Nadia's renewed illness." Queen Tiana approached a weeping willow that drooped over her long table, and touched a leaf on the tree so that all the dew began to glow to provide a little more light to the throne room. "Which was of course, quite some time ago. I imagine something new has come to pass."

"Yes, in fact," Renée replied as she played with the skirts of her light blue dress. "Jaskaran had me go and see the miracle worker in Moss Canyon. I have until the Rose Tree finishes growing its branches to become… happy I suppose."

"That doesn't sound too bad," replied Tiana as she sat at the end of the long table. She gestured for Renée to take a seat at the corner to her left. "What happens should you fail?"

"Nadia is cursed and sent to land."

"Ah, then yes you may want to change your attitude soon. The Rose Tree will be finished growing its branches in a month and a half." Tiana held her hand above the table and tea and fresh fruit appeared. "Eat something. You've lost a lot of weight."

Renée took a seat and sucked on some berries. "Why is it that everyone is on the miracle worker's side?"

"Because although you have a right to be upset about your daughter's illness, this is just ridiculous." Tiana mixed cream and sugar into her tea. "People learn to cope with sorrow instead of affecting the lives of everyone around them with it. I realize that this is something you've been battling for a while, though."

"I just don't know what it is," said Renée. "The miracle worker is right, there just seems to be something missing."

She battled the thought of telling her friend about her new concerns. Would she understand even slightly?

"I know, Renée," said Tiana. "I personally believe that if you practiced a more positive attitude, joy would soon follow."

"Well that's easier said than done," Renée informed.

"Of course it is," Tiana replied. "It would take practice. Listen, Renée, the miracle worker is very strict and unsympathetic in her ways, this is true. But what she's doing is the last chance for you and for Nadia. If the support of your friends, family, and sympathizers aren't enough, then maybe this is the push you need to realize that joy, contentment, humbleness, they are all states of mind that you find within yourself. It certainly takes time, and I understand that it'll be much harder for you than it is for most, but you also have more people willing to support you through it than most."

The empress had no reply. She quickly realized that unless she found the nerve to confide in Tiana her feelings about everyone blaming her for the illness of a child that isn't even hers, she was wasting her time looking for help here. Meanwhile, Tiana felt that she shouldn't press her luck by lecturing further.

"So how are you to know when your time is up?" Tiana asked.

"The miracle worker gave me this," Renée answered. She pulled the chain around her neck to lift the key from the bodice of her dress. "When the rose blooms, my time is up."

Queen Tiana's eyes widened at the sight of the key, but she quickly composed herself so as not to alarm

Renée. "You had better keep that well-hidden." She took a sip of tea.

"That's what the miracle worker said."

"I assume she failed to tell you why."

"She said it would hinder my search for joy."

Tiana gave an ironic chuckle as she set her teacup on the table. "Yes, I suppose it would."

"Do you know of another reason?" asked Renée.

"That key and what it unlocks is, in my personal opinion, one of the biggest mistakes us fairies have ever made. Of course, the others disagree." After adding sugar to her tea, she brought the cup back to her mouth and shrugged. "What can one do?"

"What's the mistake?" Renée eyed Tiana hungrily.

"You're aware of the myth of the Cataras Springs?" Renée nodded and Tiana shook her head. "It's no myth. It's as real as you and me. That's the key to it. Some people will kill you for that."

"I see." Renée thought for a moment. This changed *everything*. "Maybe there's a completely different reason as to why the miracle worker gave me this key."

"Like what?" Tiana asked.

"Maybe she's trying to tell me I'll find happiness there."

"She gave you a task, Renée, not a riddle."

"Sure, but don't one of the springs heal? I could… I could heal Nadia!"

"Yes, but healing your daughter won't change your mood. Otherwise, the miracle worker would've just given you medicine to heal Nadia."

"Maybe she wants me to be the one to heal Nadia. Why wouldn't that change my mood?"

"Because you've been unhappy even before you married Jaskaran. Nadia's illness only added to your negativity."

"Jaskaran and I are happily married, Tiana."

"Then perhaps you're homesick, or perhaps you require a hobby to keep your mind busy. You need to learn why you were so distraught before you got married to learn why you still feel the way you do now. Once you manage that, you can heal your mind of your condition and you'll be happier, your daughter will be in a better environment, she'll recover, and everything will be even better than before."

"I've already tried spending time with my family. As for hobbies, I quickly grow weary of them."

"Have you tried hosting galas?"

"Jaskaran hosts them. I also find them to be a bore."

"Do you go into these projects and events with this attitude?"

"I don't know, Tiana," Renée whined. "Perhaps?"

"The perhaps you can practice optimism."

"Well, I'll try the Cataras Springs first and if that fails, I'll give your advice a fair shot. Where is it?"

Tiana shook her head. "I can't tell you, Renée. You'll have to try my advice."

"Well that doesn't seem right, Tiana. I'm asking you for help."

"Who are you to tell me what's right and wrong? I must hold my tongue on the matter because I've made a covenant not to reveal its location. If you're so desperate to find the Springs, you'll have to figure it out for yourself."

"So it's just another world mystery then," said Renée. "Along with everything else you and your fairy friends created. Like what really lives at the top of the Darigo Mountains, the location of the one female miracle worker on land, if the zoilie stone exists and if it can really break any curse."

"Well, not even Aranel knows where the Mystery Miracle Worker lives. As for everything else, yes."

"Not even Aranel knows where she lives?" Renée was captivated. "How is that possible?"

"It would appear the Mystery Miracle Worker has learned how to keep Aranel from seeing her," Queen Tiana answered. "I assume either with iron or an Elvic curse."

"Fascinating. Do you suppose the Mystery Miracle Worker may know the location of the Cataras Springs?"

"I highly doubt it," Tiana replied with an amused smile. She examined Renée. "You're not planning on going out searching for her, are you?"

"It's worth a shot since you refuse to help me."

"I *am* trying to help you, Renée. That's why I'm not telling you anything. These theories you're coming up with will only waste your time!"

"Why?"

"Because the Cataras Springs can't help you! To find joy you must search for it within a given situation, not pursue it like some lost treasure!" Renée narrowed her eyes at Tiana, who could see that the fight was lost. "Very well, I will tell you this: rumor has it that someone on Arcor discovered the location of the Mystery Miracle Worker."

"Really. Do you suppose that person knows about the Springs too?"

"Absolutely not. If the location of the Springs has been found, the whole world would likely know. The many powers of the Springs are too great for anyone to keep its location secret for long, which is why I'm convinced that even the Mystery Miracle Worker doesn't know."

"Perhaps she knows, she just hasn't gone to find it."

Tiana thought for a moment. "Perhaps. Go and find the Mystery Miracle Worker, Renée. But I'm telling you right here and now, the Cataras Springs are not going to do you any good."

"We'll see about that."

With the last word, Renée stood and left the ruin. While she descended the stairs, she heard a small rustle in the tree above her followed by an excited, "Renée!" She glanced up to spot a darkly dressed, wingless pixie gazing down at her from a branch in a peach tree. "It's been a while since your last visit."

"Rein Bow," said the empress with a faint smile.

"What have you been up to lately?" Rein asked. Then her eyes fell on the key the empress was wearing. Her expression darkened. "Where did you get that?"

"A miracle worker gave it to me."

"Interesting. I suppose he didn't tell you to keep it hidden?"

Empress Renée rolled her eyes and continued descending the steps. "Everyone's been telling me."

"Why don't you listen?"

"I keep forgetting and I'm too lazy to make an effort." Rein watched the empress leave and then went to go talk to Queen Tiana about this visit.

"So she's going to Arcor?" Rein asked the queen. "With the key to the Cataras Springs?"

"I suppose so," Tiana answered with a shrug.

"How hard did you try to stop her?"

"Almost to the point of desperation, but do you really think anyone could have stopped her, Rein? She's almost as stubborn as you. Who can convince *you* to do something you don't want to do?"

Rein didn't answer. "Are you sure that an Arcorian found the Mystery Miracle Worker?"

"Positive," Tiana replied. "According to Aranel, two have. An Arcorian woman found her first and then traded the information with an Arcorian merchant."

"And does the Mystery Miracle Worker really know the location of the Springs?"

"We think so. That Arcorian woman appeared to gain the knowledge herself after visiting the Mystery Miracle Worker, and has already utilized the Springs."

Rein's eyes grew wide. "You don't say!"

Queen Tiana nodded her head. "I feel confident that once Renée is finished with the key, the Circle will vote to destroy the Cataras Springs; a feat which is long overdue."

"Do you suppose that if Renée drank from the healing spring and could bear her own child, she would be happy?" Rein asked.

"The fact that she didn't jump on the opportunity herself tells me no," Tiana answered. "Renée is angry with the world and she's in so deep that nothing but her own will could help her change her attitude. I'm hoping that by some miracle she can learn joy through this excursion she created for herself." There was a moment's pause until Tiana asked, "So what are you going to do, Rein?"

"I think I'll join her and see what I can do to help. Besides, this is the miracle worker who can give me wings again and I'm so sick of eating burdania petals every day for the last few centuries."

"Of course," said Tiana. "Good luck, Rein."

Chapter Two

Unfortunately, Rein had not yet recovered from her regrettable episode three hundred years ago when the infamous Emperor Mentir tore her wings off her back. Ever since, she had been eating the petals of the burdania flower to keep alive as pixies cannot live without wings for the most part. To further Rein's misfortune, this flower was native to the Maja Forest and when she had left this forest the first time, she had not done so on good terms. Returning without wings was humiliating, and making amends was painful. Interestingly enough, even after spending another three hundred years in the forest, not all hard feelings had been amended and Rein was anxious for this opportunity to leave again.

Throughout these years, Rein spent much of her time perfecting her hunting, running, climbing, and jumping skills. She had also tried anything and everything to keep herself distracted from her wingless predicament. Some days were easier than others, of course, though her search for a more permanent solution did wonders to keep her spirits up. It also helped to keep her nightmares at bay. It took her almost two hundred years to finally learn that she could regain wings, and it took her another hundred years to discover that the Mystery Miracle Worker was the one who could do this for her. She could hardly contain her excitement that she was finally making noticeable progress in her journey to solve this merciless problem.

To conclude her three-hundred-year-long fight, Rein experienced nightmares no more, her physical health was superior to that of her fairy friends, and she was now on her way to obtain a new set of wings. What she did have in common with the other pixies was that she now looked about the age of a twenty-year-old with a black design developing around her left eye. At this time on Xyntriav, pixies were acquiring designs on their necks and faces and they concluded it was simply a sign of age.

Rein rode a seagull to Mayline Port in the Kingdom of Belle (an island that used to be part of the Bonn Empire) where she landed outside the window of a printing press and set the bird free. She glanced around at this very modest kingdom which practiced etiquette as if it were a religion. The cobblestone streets were as clean as the people themselves and rarely did even a small argument take place. Rein didn't feel the need to worry too much about the residents here. Instead, she put all her attention in to making it to Arcor.

Rein jumped off the windowsill and ran down the alleyway between the printing press and its neighboring port operator. Rats; just like she wanted, though there were only a few considering the cleanliness of the country. Rein needed to figure out which ones had the ability to talk. Since rats usually stuck to the walls, Rein snuck down the center of the alley so to lessen the chances of being attacked by the non-talking rodents. When she found the opportunity, she quickly climbed on top of a broken crate and looked over the small colony.

"Do any of you talk?" Rein called out.

"I do," answered two rats to her left.

"Do you know if any of these ships are leaving for Arcor?"

"Lucky you," one rat replied. "There happens to be one at the west end of the port."

"More like unlucky," the second rat objected. "What business do you have in going there?"

"My business," Rein replied. Then she turned to the first one and nodded her head. "Thank you."

"No problem," he answered. "The ship is called *The Pelican*. There's a large bird on both sides of the bow so you can't miss her."

"Thanks again."

Rein jumped off the crate and ran toward the edge of the alleyway where she wondered how she could cross the street without being seen or stomped. After much deliberation, she figured that all she could do was wait for a wide opening in the traffic, pray that she wouldn't be spotted, and sprint as fast as her tiny legs could take her. She dashed bravely across the road, barely missing the hooves of a horse and the wheels of a coach. Once she made it to the other side of the road, she dove behind a stack of crates and boxes, and thanked God for a safe passage.

At this point, Rein glanced about at the ships which were docked in front of her, neither bearing the painted image of a bird of any sort. So she made her way toward the west end of the port as she peered closely at each vessel for its picture. Even though she felt safer in Belle than in most other nations, she believed it may still be wise to remain unseen in the off-chance one of the nastier citizens caught sight of her. She dodged behind barrels and kegs, crates and boxes, sacks and nets, doing all she could to keep out of sight while paying close attention to the pictures painted on these vessels. She passed about seven ships before she finally spotted *The Pelican.*

"Get those crates over there!"

Rein observed a number of shirtless, burly men working together to load the vessel with the shipment among which she hid. She concluded that was her easiest ticket on board. Rein squeezed herself between two planks of a crate and hid among the grapefruit inside. Eventually, she was carried onto *The Pelican.*

Rein remained among the cargo throughout the voyage to Arcor. It took her little time to adjust to the exaggerated swaying of the ship and the nauseating stench of fish and salty sea. For the longest time it was mostly an uneventful voyage. To keep herself occupied to some degree, Rein roamed around the area and ate some of the food along with the burdania petals she kept in her little satchel. Whenever someone came down for any reason, she hid in her crate of grapefruit and contemplated playing a harmless prank on the visitor just to add some entertainment to the journey. However, she opted not to be so foolish.

On the fourth day of the voyage, Rein heard hectic commotion on the deck above, which increased in intensity fairly quickly. It sounded frightfully war-like and Rein whispered a quick prayer that what took place above her wasn't what she thought it was. Soon, numerous footsteps barreled down the stairs to the cargo area. Rein held her breath and remained still among the fruit surrounding her.

"What be *this* madness??" exclaimed a rough voice. "Fifteen kegs of ale and thirty crates of mash! Are ya addled?"

"You gotta understand, Captain," pleaded another, smaller voice. "They wouldn't allow me to load any more than that!"

"Then ya sneak more on, fool!"

"Understood, I'll do just that next time—with extra!"

"Do ya realize how many times I've heard similar vows and never witnessed them be fulfilled?"

"Please, don't be mad!"

"Ya pathetic waste of life!" Rein heard a long, drawn-out gargle and she flinched at the following thud. "Feed this one here to the fish and get these crates on board."

"Aye, Cap'n," replied a couple of new voices.

Rein listened in panicked silence to the struggle which ensued beyond the sanctuary of her crate, then she released her breath at the relieving sound of everyone leaving the cargo area.

When the cargo bay fell silent, Rein frantically searched her mind for solutions on what to do next. Run and find a bird to ride? That would strongly depend on how far she was from Arcor and there was no way for her to find that answer. She learned during the voyage that there were no rodent holes in which to hide, and leaving the cargo area to hide elsewhere on the ship felt like the worst idea possible to her. It seemed that the safest choice was to remain in her crate and be carried onto the opposing ship. But where was that ship headed? Rein tugged at her black choppy hair in a futile effort to think harder.

About fifteen minutes passed before Rein was carried onto the other vessel. The sailors weren't very gentle about it and Rein got bruised and beat up by the grapefruit. Then once she was thrown onto the floor of the cargo bay on the new ship, she heard what sounded like the crackling of large flames and the collapsing of parts of a ship in the distance, followed by victorious praise from above. She assumed *The Pelican* was now on its way to the bottom of the ocean, and she was on her way to… well she hadn't a clue.

Moments later, a couple of sailors came below deck before she even had a chance to devise an escape plan. Yet her panic faded when she noticed that these two spoke with each other and suddenly she found herself hoping that she would be able to overhear some valuable information through their conversation.

"I really don't care," said one sailor. "I have only enemies on Arcor."

"Viroe thinks they'll come after us."

"They don't even know we sunk it, how could they come after us? Anyway, what did the cook say he wanted again? Apples, carrots, grapefruit, squash, and what else?"

"I think he said something about pears or passion fruit."

Grapefruit. That was the crate in which Rein hid. No longer was she concerned about what she could learn through their conversation. She had to find a new place to hide. She managed to escape her crate just as one of the sailors opened the lid. Rein hoped and prayed that he didn't see her light as she dove into the next crate.

"What was that?" the sailor asked.

"What was what?"

"That. Look! It just disappeared!"

"What did?"

"There was a light! Help me find where it went!"

Rein exited the new crate and dove behind a sack of potatoes. She still didn't feel safe here, so she continued to move about the cargo before she took refuge in a crate of radishes far away from the two sailors.

"What do ya mean there was a light?"

"I saw a light move! Help me find it, I'll show ya."

The two sailors searched around the crates and boxes as Rein prayed hard and constant. Then she heard them remove the lids to the boxes and search inside, swearing and coaching each other as they slowly moved closer to where she hid. She waited for what seemed like forever as they grew closer and closer still until at long last, the first sailor opened the lid to the crate of radishes.

"I found it!"

Rein bolted through the planks and the two sailors chased after her. She darted and dashed about the boxes and bags while the sailors tossed them all out of the way, fighting to snatch her up. Rein searched for any rodent holes in the walls and the more she failed to find any, the more aggravated she became. She quickly ran out of places to run, there were no places to hide, and before long Rein was cornered.

"What is it?" the second sailor asked.

It was now clear to Rein that she was a on a pirate ship, not that she had much doubt about it before she was carried on. The sailors wore baggy pants and shirts, musty from having never been washed, and they used multi-colored sashes to hold their swords at their sides.

"I can't tell," said the pirate who found her.

"Can ya talk?" asked the other. Rein nodded. "What ya be then?"

"I'm a pixie," Rein answered. "My wings were torn off."

"Ouch," said the first pirate. "That's no good. Come here."

His hands started to close in on Rein and she tried to back away from them, but she only pressed herself harder into the wall of the ship.

"No, no, no, no, no!" Rein cried. "Please! Wait! What do you want?"

"We want to show ya to the cap'n," he said.

"W-w-what's he going to do with me?"

"Can't tell," he shrugged.

"Do you know if he'll kill me?"

"Chances are, no. He ain't got reason to. Now come here."

"I found a jar!" the second pirate called out.

"No! No jars!" Rein pleaded.

"Ya won't be in there long."

"Please! I'll cooperate!"

"Ye will cooperate." The first pirate took the jar and set it in front of Rein. "By gettin' in the jar."

Rein gazed at the jar and trembled. She searched her mind for other options, areas to run off to, places to hide. Curses, if only she had wings!

"Just... don't put the lid on it?" she asked. "You know I can't fly out."

"I won't put the lid on," he swore.

Rein held on to the hope that she could reason with the captain in some way and entered the jar as instructed. The pirate lifted her off the floor with a force that caused Rein to fall the rest of the way to the bottom of the glass.

"Don't put the lid on it!" she reminded, but the pirate brought the lid up.

"No! Don't put the lid on it!"

He screwed it on.

"No! I can't breathe! I can't breathe with the lid on! Take the lid off! Please! Please take the lid off!"

The pirate carried her to the captain's cabin, the whole time ignoring Rein's shouts and pleas. When they entered the cabin, he set her on a large mahogany desk and Rein continued begging for them to remove the lid, refusing to believe that her voice was so muffled to their disregarding ears.

Once the pirates had left the cabin, Rein calmed down some but she was still panting, frustrated, frightened. She frantically searched for a way to remove the lid off the jar, but she could find none. After three hundred years, jars were made of thicker glass and she surmised that knocking it over wouldn't provide the force necessary to break it as she had managed to do last time she was trapped in something similar. She would only roll off the desk with the swaying of the ship, killing herself with the fall. All Rein could do was wait and hope that the captain would let her out when he entered and that he would enter soon.

Rein couldn't handle simply waiting, however. While the captain did whatever he pleased outside the cabin, Rein decided that it was worth a shot to climb up the inside of the jar and attempt to screw off the lid from within. She positioned her hands and feet on either side of the container and slowly pushed her way to the top where she pressed her hands beneath the lid and struggled to twist it. Her constant panting used up the little supply of oxygen left in the jar and she quickly grew tired and weak. Soon, she became incapable of holding herself at the top of the glass and her knees gave out on her. She tumbled back to the bottom of the jar just as the ship swayed, causing Rein to fall against the side so that it toppled over. Slowly, it started to roll to the edge of the captain's desk.

Chapter Three

Arcor was an ungoverned city where the most dedicated criminals came to smuggle and trade, where the outcasts came to live, and where the bloodiest of pirates came to hire their crew. This gave it a reputation for being the most unpleasant city in the world and it nearly took up the entire island.

Unlike Rein, Empress Renée was unmolested on her way to Arcor and she shored the same day as Rein was carried onto the pirate ship. The empress took cover in a snowed-out wooded area away from civilization as all the ports and beaches seemed to be in constant use by filthy, crazed Arcorians. She kept her light gray cloak wrapped tight around her and pulled her hood on to hide her streaming blonde hair and most of her face. Then she waited in the frozen air of the woods for a while where she struggled to invoke the courage required to enter the city.

Arcor's screams of terror and shouts of rage reached the empress's ears and kept her planted in her chosen spot unable to move. The only solution she could summon was that perhaps she could flow through the streets as a stream, but that would only attract more attention if someone were to spot a shimmering body of water coursing through the grimy roads. Renée paced in the crunchy snow, kicking about the black rune-like patterns the wind blew across the surface.

"What should I *do*?" she growled, pressing her fists against her temples. "Where should I go? Where do I even start *looking*?"

Turning back was not among her list of options. She had figured it all out during her journey to this large island. The world blamed her and her infertility for everything, but really, none of it was her fault. Nadia had never accepted Renée as her mother; that's why the child had always avoided her around the palace. That's why she was always ill. Renée had tried desperately to love Nadia, and she was convinced for a while that she did love Nadia. But now that she knew how everyone truly felt, resentment developed within her. She absolutely had to enter this city to find the merchant who knew where she could locate the Mystery Miracle Worker. If Renée found the Cataras Springs and drank from the Spring of Healing herself, she could bear her own children who would love her and prove to everyone that she was a good mother. And then, of course, she could bring some of the water to Nadia since she was still, after all, the heir to the throne.

After a couple more minutes of pacing and speaking to herself, Renée focused harder to gather the strength to enter Arcor. She cautiously approached the edge of the wood and peeked out from behind a tall, skinny gray tree. She caught sight of the ratty townsfolk arguing, trading, stealing, drinking, fighting, singing, vandalizing, anything and everything that would be considered careless or even lawless anywhere. She hesitated again, then conjured up some water from the snow and formed it into a dagger to keep with her for an emergency. Finally, with a deep breath to calm her frenzied nerves, Renée entered the unholy city of Arcor.

The empress kept to the center of the street where there was less commotion. Every once in while she had to dodge people fighting, people stumbling drunk, people fleeting. She was even almost run down by rampant horses towing a carriage where the product it held was aflame. Death and violence surrounded her and it filled the air with the odors of sweat, rust, and decay. It was clear to Renée that no one bothered to rid the streets of the putrid bodies and rotting trash anymore. The red blood and black muck mingled with the brown snow on the ground and buildings. She had learned through a rumor that whatever rules existed were unwritten and they happened to be mainly trading rules, such as, "I'll give you something if you give me something in return." There was also one peace rule: "Don't bother me, I won't destroy you." But since all who came to Arcor were narcissistic to say the least, these rules were often completely disregarded and she made sure to keep this in mind.

To Renée's surprise, few of these people paid her any mind, but this was probably because many found it easier to snatch the attentions of the willing promiscuous women who coaxed them from the balconies of some of the rarer sturdy buildings. Yet there were a few Arcorians who took a moment from whatever they were doing to stare at Renée suspiciously, but no one bothered to approach her until she passed a tavern where one drunken satyr was thrown out. In a sputter of profanities, he stumbled into Renée and nearly knocked her into the sloshy ground.

"So sorry, my Lady," he slurred. "But you were too delicious to resist. Come with me and I'll show you how to have a good time!"

"How dare you!" Renée spat as she pushed him away.

"Oh! You're one of *those* types, huh?" the satyr laughed.

"Unhand me!" Renée hurled the satyr to the icy mud. "Curse you and your entire race!"

"Oy!" he cried, enraged. "Nobody shoves *me*!"

Suddenly, a number of his satyr friends exited the same tavern and waved their mugs around, spouting unintelligible words, though Renée managed to make out a few sentences.

"Oy! What are you doing shoving my friend?"

"Come try sssshoving one of us and see what happens!"

"Go shove someone your own size!"

Renée scampered away before they decided to come after her, and as she took off, they gave chase. However, their hooves didn't tread well with the icy ground and they quickly tumbled on top of each other and their friend. Renée didn't bother stopping, and it wasn't until she turned a corner that she decided to peek out from behind the building and see if the drunken satyrs had progressed at all. She was thankful to find that they had already forgotten about her when they all ended up in the mud, and were pointing and laughing at each other.

This newfound relief did little to calm the anxiety which emanated from the city around Renée. She glanced about at her dilapidated bearings, her eyes bouncing from ruin to trash heap to dead tree to another ruin. At last, across the street she spotted a crusty sign above a door bearing a picture of a book. It was the city library, depreciated and apparently unused. Perhaps she could find some useful information on the Mystery Miracle Worker inside.

The empress scuffled across the street through the smoky air and entered the library, and what she found was very discouraging. There were many shelves and bookcases, but there were hardly any books to be seen. The books she did find were poorly taken care of; they were dusty, missing pages, missing *covers*, and the bindings were falling apart. In addition, the librarian was nowhere to be found, which was fine with Renée. The last thing she needed was another dicey encounter to slow her down.

Renée quietly strolled up and down the aisles even though she didn't know where to remotely begin her search. Since there weren't many options, she thought to glance at the books until one stood out as having some potential. Besides her soft footsteps, the quiet surrounding her sent goosebumps creeping up her skin. However, Renée found that she had preferred the quiet when she suddenly heard a second pair of slow and steady footsteps coming from behind the bookcase she stood beside. They crept to the end of the aisle and turned the corner to reveal the mysterious stalker. It was who Renée assumed to be the librarian: an old, fat, clay golem. Golems were mainly used as slaves on land, and because the librarian was a golem, Empress Renée immediately felt great contempt toward her. She almost decided to walk out of the library and forget about looking for the Mystery Miracle Worker there.

"What are you doing here?" the librarian asked. It was clear that she too felt disdain toward Renée. "I don't tolerate trespassers."

"Are libraries not open to the public?" Renée asked.

"This hasn't been a library for years," the golem answered. "It is my home now, and you're trespassing."

"I'm searching a library for information."

"You won't find any information here."

Renée hesitated for a moment. She didn't wish to speak to the golem anymore, but her search was too important to give up. "Very well. Then would you happen to know where I could find the Mystery Miracle Worker? Or perhaps the merchant who knows her whereabouts?"

The golem laughed. "Is that what you're looking for?"

Renée showed little physical response to being mocked, but it was all she could do to keep from drowning the golem. "Yes."

The golem tilted her head at the empress. "What do I get out of giving you that information?"

Renée took a moment to think. Her malicious feelings toward this simpleton were only increasing at a rapid pace.

"I can pay you." Pay a golem? That phrase left a bitter taste in her mouth.

"How much?"

"How much would you like?" Renée asked through gnashed teeth.

"How much do you have?"

The empress was ready to explode on this slave-material. The golem should be thankful she was getting anything at all. Renée molded some gold coins out of the water particles in the air behind her back before showing them to the librarian. "I have… a full moon." A hundred dollars.

"Crescents don't do anything here."

"Except for the fact that they're pure gold, which does something everywhere."

The golem's eyes widened and she reached out for the money. Renée quickly pulled back and made sure her words were comprehensible when she asked, "Where can I find information on the Mystery Miracle Worker?"

The golem glared at Renée. "The merchant seadog you're looking for is several shops from here. I don't know if he's there at the moment since he *is* a seadog."

"What's the name of the shop?"

"Worldly Trade. There's a picture of Xyntriav above his door."

Renée considered her answer. She didn't like how vague the information was, but what could she do? Perhaps this was all that this useless golem could provide, which shouldn't surprise her. Reluctantly, she handed the money over.

"If I find this information to be false, I will come back for this money. If it's not here, I'll take the payment in some *other* way, if you catch my drift." With that said, Empress Renée left the library.

Renée glanced up and down the street to avoid any trouble-seekers before she rushed away from the rickety structure. She hopped over broken wood planks and severed body parts as she kept close to the deteriorating buildings, guardedly making her way down the street and being sure to keep an eye out for any unruly citizens. She found the little, "Worldly Trade" shop just as run-down as the library, but she found it open and she felt a rush of relief to get off the streets again. Dealing with one or two rowdy people was way preferable to dealing with an entire chaotic city. She entered the shop and looked around for whoever might be inside but only saw a large desk, a bunch of maps, and a variety strange objects used for voyages and navigation.

"And what might someone like yourself be looking for in a shop like this?" came a voice from behind.

Renée spun around to find a man standing by the door with his arms crossed over his chest. She looked at him directly and hesitated to speak when she saw his feet were on backward. She had never heard of an abarimon before, so she didn't understand that this was only normal for his ethnicity.

"I'm looking for the merchant who I was told works here," she uttered.

"What do you want from him?"

"That is between me and him."

"Is he expecting you?"

"No..."

"Then you must go through me first. What is it you're looking for?"

"The location of a certain someone," Renée answered. "And that is all you're going to get out of me."

"And what if I told you that I'm the merchant you want?"

"I wouldn't believe you for a second. Now if you would, I'd like to speak with him."

The abarimon laughed and he approached his desk to pack up the maps spread out on top of it. "I'm afraid, my dear, I am the person you wish to speak to. However, I'm pressed on time, so we must hurry with your business so that I may go."

"Prove it to me that you are who I search for," Renée demanded as she placed her hand on her hips.

"I'm afraid that's not possible," said the merchant as he placed the maps against the wall beside a bookcase. "Now either you can ask me what you want or I'm going to leave." The merchant approached his door to exit.

"I'm looking for the Mystery Miracle Worker," Renée spat.

The merchant paused and closed his door. "What business do you have looking for her?"

"Now that business is between her and myself, and there is no way you could possibly convince me that you are her, so there's no point in trying."

"Right," said the merchant as he crossed his arms again and leaned leisurely against the door. "But I will ask for something in return for this information."

Renée rolled her eyes. "Everybody wants something! What is it you'd like?"

"That key you so carelessly wear like a steel chain around your neck," the merchant answered.

Renée put her hand over the key and tucked it into the blouse of her dress. "The key is off limits. What else do you wish for?"

"Nothing else. It's the key or no information. Make your choice, and quickly please."

Renée thought fast. "Very well, but you will only receive the key when you have told me everything I need to know. I can't trust that you'll tell me once I give it to you."

"Well then we seem to be at a stalemate as I can't trust that I'll get the key after I reveal the location," the abarimon replied.

"It seems as though we cannot reach an accord. Thank you for your time. I must go and find the information I seek elsewhere."

Renée approached the door to leave the shop, but the merchant stopped her. "Hold on," he said. "We'll do this your way. Unfortunately though, the information you want is at my home on the other side of the city, which is a day's journey from here. If you give me until tomorrow, I shall return here by noon with everything you need know. Then we can make trade. What do you say?"

Finally, Renée was getting somewhere. "I'll be here at noon."

Chapter Four

The two pirates who had taken Rein captive returned to the cabin with the captain just as the jar containing Rein began to tumble off the desk. Immediately the captain dove for the jar and caught it just moments before it shattered on the floor.

"What did ya do?" the captain scolded as he brought himself back to his feet.

"We left the jar on the desk so it wouldn't roll like that, Cap'n," the first pirate said. "She musta did that herself."

The second pirate observed Rein closely. "She don't look so good."

"You fools!" the captain exclaimed as he removed the lid. "She's suffocating 'cause ya put the lid on the jar!" He poured the limp pixie into his hand and set the jar on his desk. "Return to yer posts, ya bottle-heads."

"Aye, Cap'n," they both replied shamefully.

The captain laid Rein on his desk and waited for her to regain her strength. "Can ya hear me, Little Pixie?" he asked.

Rein's head buzzed in sync with her fuzzy vision. She glanced around in search for the owner of the voice speaking to her. "Please," Rein managed to say between breaths. "Don't..."

"I ain't gonna hurt ya," the captain assured as he took his seat behind his desk. Now she could see who spoke to her, though he appeared as a large, red and brown blur. "I just wanna talk to ya. But if ya need yer rest, I completely understand."

"What will happen... if I sleep?" Rein asked as her vision only depleted further.

"Absolutely nothing. Again, I wanna talk to ya."

"I don't want... to sleep..." and then the world went black.

Rein awoke to find herself most comfortable on a velvet handkerchief placed inside an ornate ebony cigar case. She slowly sat up inside and took a moment to gather where she was, how she got there, and why she was there. Then, she quietly peered through the keyhole to see what was happening outside, but was unable to conclude anything besides the fact that she was still on the captain's desk. She poked her head out of the keyhole and glanced around some more.

The cabin was elegant for a pirate captain. The entire ship appeared to be made of redwood—a great material for ship-building on Xyntriav. It also released a faint scent of forest that mixed beautifully with that of saltwater. It seemed the captain was well-read as he had two bookcases filled to the brim with books. Due to the windows being stained glass and draped with cotton, mahogany curtains, as well as the quality furniture and abundance of treasures which decorated the cabin, Rein could tell that the captain had refined taste. Then judging by the pieces that represented his many rumored adventures, Rein came to the accurate conclusion that she was trapped on the *Blood Omen*: the ship of the infamous Captain Tzatara. It was said that he had never been defeated and that he had found at least two Xyntriav World Wonders, making him the most respected and feared pirate in the world.

Rein was about to attempt to squeeze through the keyhole of the box in which she was encased when she heard the cabin doors open to a conversation between the captain and one of his crew. She quickly ducked back inside and listened closely.

"Ya don't understand, Cap'n," said the voice of the crew member. "We must do something before someone on Arcor finds out about *The Pelican*."

"They won't find out," replied the captain. "Unless a sea rat from our boat blabs when we return."

"And what about the supplies? What's Arcor gonna do?"

"When *The Pelican* doesn't make berth, they'll send for another cargo ship."

Rein saw the captain sit in his chair and the voice of whom Rein assumed to be the first mate was now closer on the other side of the desk.

"But there still won't be any supplies for a while. It takes weeks for another shipment to be ready. We have the supplies Arcor needs."

"Arcor will survive. They'll just go without much rum for a while. It wouldn't be any different if *The Pelican* was lost in a storm in the middle of its voyage."

"Chaos will erupt, Cap'n."

"And we won't be there to witness it." The captain grinned.

"But what about our mates on the island?"

"Since when did ya bear such a kind heart, Yacomé?" the captain asked.

"I'm just worried about our port, Cap'n. When we dock again, will there be an Arcor left? And if so, will our mates welcome us back?"

"Of course there will be an Arcor left! And they'll welcome us because they won't know that we commandeered their supplies."

"Ya know what I mean, Cap'n."

"Well ya shouldn't worry so much. Since we have a lot more cargo on this boat, we won't be docking *anywhere* for some time. So any problem Arcor may have will be taken care of by the time we dock again. Now I can continue to search for… what I've been searching for, without having to stop for supplies."

Rein caught the captain's fleeting glance at the cigar case with his piercing green eyes.

"We won't be docking for… *how* long?" Yacomé asked.

"I reckon we won't be docking for, at least, another three months perhaps," the captain answered. "At most six months. Yer enough of a seadog to be able to handle such a voyage, I hope?"

"Aye, Cap'n."

"Good. Now get back to yer post. And tell the crew that I don't want to be disturbed for the next hour or so."

"Aye, Cap'n."

Rein heard the footsteps of the first mate leave and the cabin doors close. Then the captain took out his ring of keys, so Rein moved away from the keyhole and sunk low into the handkerchief. The captain unlocked the box and opened it a crack, just enough to see if Rein was awake.

"Are ya gonna try to scurry off?" the captain asked her. "Or can I open this all the way?"

Rein didn't answer, but only sank further into the handkerchief. Her mind raced with potential escape routes, but it was difficult to determine the effectiveness of her plans in what felt like such a short period of time.

"Are ya gonna stay put?" the captain asked again.

Rein nodded, so the captain opened the box.

"Now stay in the box. I'm just gonna ask ya some questions and I want honest answers. Can ya do that for me?"

Even though she had an idea as to the type of questions the captain wished to ask her, Rein nodded again. She sat up a little and looked around outside the box to verify possible escape routes again.

"Good," said the captain. "So how did ya get on me boat? Stay in the box…"

Rein sank back into the handkerchief. Was she caught? Did he figure out what she was doing?

"Relax, Little Pixie. I ain't gonna hurt ya," the captain reassured. "What's yer name, for starters?"

Rein hesitated but answered quietly with a cracked voice, "Rein Bow. Two words."

"Hello, Rein," the captain said. "I'm Captain Tzatara. Now, how did ya get on me boat?"

"I stowed away on *The Pelican* by hopping into a crate of grapefruit," Rein answered. "Then your crew carried me on."

"I see," said Captain Tzatara. "My men tell me your wings were torn off some time ago."

"By Emperor Mentir over three hundred years ago," Rein answered.

"You've lived over three hundred years without wings?"

"Yes, sir. I've been living off the burdania flower."

"Ah, I see." Captain Tzatara stroked his raggedy red-brown beard in thought. "So ya hid yerself on *The Pelican,* eh? Did ya know where to it was headed?"

"Yes, sir."

"You want to go to Arcor?"

Rein nodded.

"Ya do know that Arcor isn't necessarily a vacation spot, right?"

Rein nodded again.

"And that's where ya were headed?"

Rein nodded once more.

"Well speak to me, Little Pixie!" the captain laughed.

"My friend is there," Rein said finally.

"Ah. Might I know yer friend?"

"No, she doesn't live there. It's a long story, sir."

"I see. Yer not dressed very well to be going to Arcor, ya know. It be winter there."

Rein looked at what she was wearing: a crimson tube-top and a tight skirt of blackflower petals, which ended a little above her knees revealing diamond markings on her right calf and strange etchings on her left thigh. Under the tube-top, she wore a long-sleeved fishnet shirt. A gold chain was wrapped around her hip as a belt and a holder for her dagger and rope. Finally, she wore black slippers and fingerless gloves.

"I realize that," Rein answered. "But the journey was last-minute and I had no time to change."

"Well fortunately for you," Captain Tzatara said as he rose from his seat, "I happen to have a collection of sprite outfits stashed away for ya to rummage through and pick out what ya fancy."

Rein watched Captain Tzatara walk across the cabin and open the dark purple cushion of his window-seat. He brought out a tiny jewelry box with geometric designs skillfully carved into the black wood.

"What do you want in return?" Rein asked.

Captain Tzatara shrugged as he brought the box back to his desk. "Nothing, it's not like I have need for them."

Rein leaned out of the cigar case to get a closer look at the box the captain had set in front of her. Then she looked back at him. "Am I allowed out, Captain?"

Captain Tzatara nodded. "Just don't scurry off."

Rein climbed out of the cigar case and approached the box. Inside was just about everything, from pants to cloaks, to shoes and accessories.

"What all am I allowed to take?" Rein asked.

"Whatever ye can carry, my dear," the captain laughed. "Again, I don't need them."

"There must be a catch."

"The catch will come with a different offering I plan to give ya later, my dear. But right now, just enjoy yerself. This is my way of showing that ya can trust me."

Rein wondered how he got his hands on this jewelry box full of sprite and pixie clothes, but she shook all possible answers out of her mind and tried to do what Captain Tzatara said: enjoy the gift. She searched through the lot and picked whatever struck her as her. She pulled out a black velvet coat and held it up to the light. It resembled a pirate's coat, but she loved how soft and warm it felt inside when she put it on.

"Suits ye," Captain Tzatara complimented.

Rein continued to dig through the box until she was distracted by something shimmering under a pink skirt. She grabbed it by the hilt and held it in front of her. It was a sword complete with its sheath.

"It's a beauty ain't it?" Captain Tzatara commented. "I wish there be one my size. Know how to use one?"

"Somewhat."

Rein shrugged and set the sword aside to continue searching through the clothing. She brought out a pair of black leather boots with squirrel fur inside. They fit her well enough. Then came the dark purple, long-sleeved wool shirt with gold floral designs embroidered by pixies themselves. Rein pulled it over the shirts she currently wore.

"Ya do know that you can get yer wings back, right?" Captain Tzatara finally asked.

Rein glanced at the captain, guessing where this statement was going to lead. She knew that the end of the upcoming conversation would not be pleasant.

"Yes, I found out a hundred twenty-three years ago." She continued to search through the box. "Apparently only the Mystery Miracle Worker can do it. No one can find her though, hence her name."

"She's very well-hidden indeed," Captain Tzatara acknowledged as he stood up.

Rein pulled a pair of crimson, cotton leggings from the box and watched as the captain approached his bookshelf. He removed a leather-bound book, rather small in size.

"She told me that she wanted to find a place no one could find in a million years," he continued as he returned to his desk. "Seems to me that she's quite succeeded in that, for the most part."

Rein watched as Captain Tzatara opened the cover of the book and she caught a passing glimpse of what appeared to be a loose first page.

"You know her?" Rein asked as she slipped the leggings on underneath her skirt. They were a little long for her, but they would suffice.

"We were lovers once," the captain said after he sat back down at his desk.

"So, you know where she lives?"

"Aye. Every detail."

Rein found herself predicting almost each step of this entire conversation while she put the boots back on. "This is where the catch comes in isn't it?"

"Yer absolutely right, my dear," Captain Tzatara said. "I want something in return if I'm going to tell ya where she be."

Rein shrugged on the black coat. "Well, luckily for me, someone on Arcor knows where she lives, so I can just ask that person."

"Chances are they only vaguely know where she lives. But there be more important details you'll need in order to find her exact whereabouts."

Rein narrowed her eyes at the captain. "What do you mean?"

"For instance, she lives inside a cave that be located inside another cave. What be the chances of this Arcorian knowing that much and more?"

Rein was skeptical, but Captain Tzatara was most likely correct. It couldn't be easy to find the Mystery Miracle Worker, or else everyone would have found her by now. It was possible that the Arcorian merchant may have an idea as to where the Mystery Miracle Worker was located, but unless he had paid her a visit, he likely knew little details. While if the captain had known her personally at one point in time, he would have all the information Rein needed.

"What exactly do you want for the extra details?" Rein asked. "I don't have much to offer."

"Ah, but ye have plenty to offer. Yer a pixie!"

Rein could feel her blood pressure rise, even though this was precisely how she had expected this conversation to go. "It's very unfortunate how strong my weakness is."

"Aye," said the captain. "I can understand that sentiment."

"I can't tell you anything, Captain. I've sworn an oath."

"Ya don't even know what I'm gonna ask yet."

Rein swallowed her panic. "So tell me."

Rein bit her hand and refused to look at Captain Tzatara as he explained what he wanted to know. She wasn't surprised.

"Ya see, Rein Bow, I've been searching several years now for the key to the Cataras Springs."

Chapter Five

Rein buried her face in her hands. All species of fairies had witnessed the creation of Xyntriav and they knew of all the wonders of the world… almost every detail. For instance, they knew how the Cataras Springs worked, they knew about the two keys allotting people inside, and they were aware of the three entryways which existed.

"What interest, exactly, do you have in the Cataras Springs?" Rein asked as she sat on the edge of the cigar case.

"I desire to drink the waters of the Spring of Agelessness," answered the captain.

"You do realize it is only agelessness you will receive and not immortality."

"I do realize this," he replied. "But it be agelessness I want and not immortality. If I wanted immortality, I would not be seeking the Cataras Springs."

"I suppose not." Rein racked her mind for more ways out, or at least ways to stall. "Why don't you want immortality? With agelessness you can still be killed but with immortality, you won't die *ever.*"

"Which takes away all the excitement I experience every day in the sweet trade. There be more thrill involved in piracy than just thieving and killing, my dear."

Rein rubbed her forehead and sighed.

"So, are ya gonna tell me?" the captain pressed.

Rein didn't reply. She didn't even look at him. Her heart sank with every second that went by without a solution.

"Well then, I guess ye won't be gettin' yer wings back."

Captain Tzatara rose from his seat and left the cabin after returning his book to the bookcase. Rein gazed up at the ceiling with another sigh and sat defeated in the same spot, her elbows on her knees. What could she do to get this information from the captain without giving away the location of the key?

Hours later, Rein lay in the open cigar case staring into space, still searching for solutions to this newfound problem. Now and then, she glanced out the window for any sign of birds or land, but it appeared they still sailed too far out in the ocean. She longed to explore the cabin for answers or perhaps something that could spark a useful thought, but for how long would the captain be gone? What would happen if he returned and caught her snooping about?

Eventually, Rein had grown so restless that she left the cigar case and stood at the edge of the desk where she scanned the cabin. The captain couldn't get upset at her for going such a short distance, right? Surely he could understand her desire to not be trapped in a single spot for hours on end? Of course, finding the nerve to go this far inspired the temptation to proceed just a little farther. Rein glanced around for a means to get off the desk, and that was when she heard someone approach the cabin doors. Too bad she hadn't found this courage an hour or so ago. Rein took a seat at the edge of the desk and placed her head in her hand to make it appear as though she was perhaps bored, and not plotting anything suspicious.

Captain Tzatara entered with a plate of food in his hand and approached his desk without a word. Rein found his apparent indifference about her being out of the cigar case relieving. He sat in his fancy gold and burgundy seat where he then tore off a piece of bread and set it in front of Rein.

"Ya hungry? If ya don't want bread, I have fruit and meat here. Ye can have whatever ya like."

Rein acted as if she didn't even hear the captain, which was difficult as she was very hungry and the aroma of freshly cooked meat was not easy to ignore.

"Ya know," continued the captain, "ye can still tell me where the key be. It's not as though the deal's off."

"Listen," Rein said as she got up and took a grape from his plate. She couldn't resist the food any longer. "Someone else is using the key right now. Not for the Springs though. She's been given a task and only has a certain amount of time to complete it. The key tells her how much longer she has. So I can't give it to you right now, even if I wanted to."

"I see," the captain said. "That's quite the predicament, ain't it? That's too bad."

Rein felt her hackles rise at incredible speed. Clearly Captain Tzatara still wanted her to tell him where the key was. Couldn't he ask for something else? Rein forced her rage back down with a deep breath.

"Out of curiosity, why aren't you asking where the Springs are located?"

"I be on my way to talk to someone about that right now," the captain answered.

"I can save you the trip," Rein offered after swallowing a bit of her grape.

"No, I want *you* to give me the key. Because even if I knew the location of the Springs, the key be the only way I can enter."

Rein paused and thought for a second. This wasn't entirely true, but telling him about the other two entrances wouldn't help either of them, so there was no point. She had to come up with something else.

"What if I told you about all the wonders of the Springs?"

"I already know about them."

Rein failed hide her shock. "What?"

"I already know about them," the captain repeated. He took a large a bite of his meat and smiled behind his scruffy facial hair.

"Then what are they?" Rein challenged.

"There be thirteen of them," Captain Tzatara began as he leaned back in his seat and brushed his hands together. "The Spring of Agelessness, the Spring of Youth, of healing, wisdom, beauty, knowledge, power, life, strength, complete rule, wealth, freedom, and lastly the Spring of Ultimacy. And before ya bother, I do know how the Springs work. At the entrance of the realm, there be thirteen goblets of different colors, one goblet to each spring. The trick be that ya have to match the right goblet to the right spring. The more extraordinary the wonder, the harder it be to find. Ye know ya found the right one when the goblet ya hold disappears in the water. And trust me, I know which goblet goes to which spring and the details of what spring does what. Please don't make me name 'em."

Rein gaped blankly at the captain. "How do you know all this?"

Captain Tzatara smiled and got up to fetch another book from his bookcase. This volume stood out from all the others on the shelf. The cover was made from ebony and had gold designs etched into the wood. The pages were aged and lined with gold dust and the bookmark was of violet velvet. The captain opened the book in front of Rein and she knew exactly which book it was without having to read its glistening title: *Xyntriav Book of Wonders.*

"How did you find this?" Rein asked as she peered wide-eyed at its contents. The pictures inside moved and had sound and color. It was awe-inspiring. Sure, Rein was aware of its existence, but she had never seen it before.

"La Tennaco Canyon," Captain Tzatara answered. "Obviously, it wasn't an easy prize. Especially since I didn't have the help that it offers to find it. Unfortunately, the fairies were clever enough to leave out some important information and that's where you come in."

Rein snapped out of her amazement. "I can finish it for you," she offered as she turned back to the first page. The Fairy Circle would have her drawn and quartered, but if she obtained wings again, she would never have to return to the Maja Forest and they would never try and convict her. "I can answer all the questions this book leaves you with."

Captain Tzatara stopped her by closing the book. "Ye can start with the location of the key."

"Well, everything besides that of course," Rein said.

The captain pulled the book away from her. "I don't care about everything else at the moment. I want the key."

"But you might want to know for future reference," Rein suggested.

"Then I'll figure it all out in the future. Right now, I'm more worried about the present."

"Captain! Captain!" A crewmember pounded on the cabin door.

"Get in the box," the captain ordered.

Rein decided that it would be more sensible to obey the captain's every word in order to stay on his good side. In making that decision, she immediately hopped into the cigar case and let the captain close and lock it.

"Captain! We've come upon the *Royal Marina*!"

"Is that so..."

Rein heard the captain rush out of the cabin and lock the doors behind him. Then came a series of shouts and cheers from the deck. Rein sulked in the case and crumpled the velvet kerchief in her tight fists. How could she learn the information she needed to get her wings back without telling the captain that Empress Renée had the key on Arcor? She remembered the small, leather-bound book that Captain Tzatara had shown her and realized that this time, she had an estimate to how long the captain may be out of his cabin.

The *Royal Marina* was a ship that transported the royal family of the wealthy country of Vira. Captain Tzatara wouldn't let an opportunity like that slip his grasp, and the chances of the *Royal Marina* surviving his attack were slim as he had the reputation of domination around the world. So, Rein concluded that she had plenty of time to get a lot done and no fear of death during the captain's fight.

Rein slipped out the keyhole of the cigar box and gazed at the bookcase where she found the book she desired three shelves up from the bottom. She glanced around for a way off the desk, jumped down onto the captain's chair, and then to the floor. She would figure out how to get back onto the desk later. Meanwhile outside the cabin, Rein could hear Captain Tzatara and his crew shout, jeer, and taunt the crew of the *Royal Marina*. They hadn't attacked yet. She darted across the floor and heard the captain shout orders at his crew the moment she reached the foot of the bookcase. The uproar on deck grew louder and with trembling limbs, Rein began her climb to the third shelf. The sound of war only increased her anxiety, but Rein continued on with her mission and worked to climb faster.

Soon after she reached her destination, two men collided into the cabin doors, grunting and growling at each other as they tried to wrestle the weapons out of the hands of their rivals. Rein pressed herself into the side of the bookcase in anticipation for the doors to break open, but they held firm. Finally, she heard what she concluded to be the sounds of one man stabbing the other and leaving him to die at the threshold, though she couldn't be sure through the colored, dirty glass who was on what side. With no small amount of effort, Rein forced herself to forget what she had witnessed and continued to pursue her commodity. She drew close to the line of books and journals and used them as support to keep herself from falling off the shelf until she finally reached the book she was after. Now the trick was removing and opening it safely.

Before Rein could decide how to access the book, the two warring ships started to catapult each other with large boulders, nearly knocking her off the shelf with the sheer force of every collision. As the impacts continued, each new boulder seemed to make its mark with increasing power. Rein watched as some of the captain's precious objects tumbled to the floor, including his books. She gripped one of these volumes desperately and when it became dislodged from its spot on the shelf, she shifted to grasp a journal. But a boulder collided with the *Blood Omen* before she had a firm hold of the journal's spine and she plummeted from the shelf back to the base of the bookcase. More volumes and diaries fell after her and she was forced to roll away before she could even clear her head from its impact with the floor.

To Rein's relief, one of the objects which fell was the small leather-bound book she wanted access to anyway. As she kept an eye out for more tumbling reading material, she opened the cover and found a folded piece of parchment inside it. Was this the loose piece she had eyed previously? Rein frantically opened the aged page and flattened it with her shivering hands to observe the map of an island. Then Rein's heart dropped when she noticed something that was quite unfortunate—the words were written in a language with which she was not fluent.

Rein was forced to spend more time studying the writing to figure out what language it was. It wasn't an elf language, a dwarf language, or the native language of the Continent Islands chain. It was Captain Tzatara's map, where was Captain Tzatara from? What language was the name "Tzatara?" Rein knew it meant, "great leader," in some language, but *what language*? She finally managed to organize her scrambled thoughts and narrowed her choices down to two: Hagorian and Dovish. The problem now was that those two languages were very similar and almost identical when written. However, there were times when they were strictly different, and usually during very important times—for instance, when reading maps.

Rein only knew a little of both languages, so she racked her mind to decipher which island was depicted on this parchment. Hopefully, that would help her to confirm the language. After several ship-wracking boulder blasts, Rein concluded that she was looking at a map of Roznova and the language was Dovish. Roznova was in fact one of the Continent Islands. This was convenient since she had already been headed to Arcor, the largest island on the chain, which meant that she and the empress wouldn't necessarily have to travel far after they met up.

Suddenly, the catapults ceased, signaling the end of the battle and cheers erupted on deck. Rein quickly stuffed the map between the pages of the book and scrambled to decide if she should try to return to the desk or if she should hide somewhere nearby. She examined the smooth wooden legs of both the chair and the desk and rapidly established they were too smooth for her to climb. Rein listened as the cheers outside calmed and the ringing in her ears claimed her hearing. Was it possible that she could hide somewhere in the cabin until they neared land? Rein doubted this but she could produce few other options. She spotted a trinket box carved into the shape of a tiny treasure chest on the first shelf of the bookcase behind her. She threw open the lid to find pearls and gold chains inside. Desperate, Rein climbed in, covered herself in the gold and gems, and shut the lid over her.

Moments later, Rein heard the cabin door unlock and the familiar sound of the captain's laughter followed.

"Go loot the boat and sink it! Take no prisoners!"

The doors closed and locked again. Rein remained completely motionless.

"So, Little Pixie. Where were we in our delightful conversation before I conquered the *Royal Marina*?"

Rein listened intently as the captain unlocked the cigar box on his desk. Her head buzzed and her breathing became quick and shallow.

"What the—Rein?" The captain's voice was firm. "I know yer still in here somewhere. You'd better reveal yerself before ya get in more trouble when I find ya."

Rein stayed quiet. She shivered among the jewels as the air grew hot in the tiny box. Meanwhile, the captain shuffled about the cabin, moving things around and swearing under his breath. The tension grew so difficult to bear that Rein even contemplated revealing herself in the hopes of gaining mercy, but she couldn't decide for certain if that was a wise decision.

"If I were this little pixie, where would I be?" Captain Tzatara asked aloud.

In the darkness of the box, Rein could hear footsteps nearing her hideout. Slowly. Cautiously.

"Hmmm…"

Suddenly, light flooded into the box and surrounded Rein.

Chapter Six

Rein jumped back with a yelp and kept low in the trinket box. She couldn't bring herself to look Captain Tzatara in the eye as he gazed down at her with an expression on his face which she couldn't read.

"There ya are, Little Pixie."

Rein had no way to reply. She thought about begging for mercy, but quickly ruled that out as pointless. Without a word, the captain held out his large, musty hand for Rein to climb onto it. She hesitated and looked back and forth from the captain to his filthy hand. Finally, she reminded herself that it might be wise to cooperate.

"Now, ya know I have to punish ya for that," Captain Tzatara said as he carried Rein back to his desk.

Rein hated the way his tone implied that he didn't want to punish her. He played as though he was the nice guy, and it was all she could do not to scream how she wasn't the simpleton he thought her to be.

"But how honest ya are about what ya learned from the map will determine how merciful yer punishment will be," Captain Tzatara continued. He let Rein off his hand and onto his desk.

Rein glanced at the leather-bound book on the floor with the map sticking out beneath the cover. She had failed to hide her tracks well enough. She silently kicked herself and then addressed the captain. "You won't believe me if I tell you the truth."

"Well let's see," said the captain as he got comfortable in his chair. "Try me."

Rein dropped her arms at her side in defeat. "I only know four languages fluently, Captain: Noelle, Northern Elvish, Atlikan, and Roshirian. I know only a little of other languages and I am hardly literate in any. I swear I only managed to learn that the language is Dovish and that it's a map of Roznova. Truly, that's all I know."

The captain thought for a moment. "Very well, I'll be merciful." He grabbed the same jar that Rein was trapped in before and placed it in front of her. "Get in the jar."

Rein took a tentative step back. "This is merciful?"

"Would ya like to know the other punishment I had in mind?"

Rein hesitated. "No."

"I thought so. Get in the jar."

"You're not going to put the lid on it, are you?"

"I swear I will not."

Rein swallowed her panic as she entered the jar. Then Captain Tzatara lifted it off the desk and Rein slid to the bottom.

"Don't put the lid on!" Rein pleaded.

"I swore I wouldn't," said the captain. He set the jar upright between the cigar case and a globe so that she wouldn't be able to knock it over. Then he stood from his seat and left the cabin without another word.

Once Captain Tzatara had left, Rein gazed up through the opening of the jar with the knowledge that she could climb out if she really wanted. It would be difficult, but she had managed to reach the lid last time she was trapped inside this very container. Though, what would be the point? There was no way for her to leave the ship and she would eventually be found if she tried to hide.

Rein was fully aware that this was a tease. If she had wings, she'd easily be able to fly out of the jar, perhaps perch atop a mast, and wait to leave until they sailed by any speck of land. Indeed, the captain was clever. He knew this would be the perfect persuasion to force Rein to ponder the necessity of wings, which would push her to tell him what he wanted to know. He probably had no other punishment in mind; this would have been it whether she had told him the truth or not.

Rein sat against the side of the jar and searched her mind for solutions yet again. She tapped her head against the glass thinking, fighting, striving, and desperately reaching. At long last, an idea dawned on her and she had to tell the captain immediately.

"Captain!" she shouted and thrashed her fists against the container. "Captain!" Rein took a long, deep breath and shouted as loud as she could manage, "*Captain!!*"

However, her attempts were futile. Rein considered climbing out of the glass and pounding against the door of the cabin, but she recalled that the captain had made efforts to keep her secret from his crew, so perhaps that wasn't a wise decision. She would have to be patient and wait for his return to voice her idea. With a heavy sigh, Rein slumped back down in her prison and threw her head against the glass in frustration. To her dismay, Captain Tzatara failed to return for several hours and during the wait, Rein eventually fell asleep.

The next morning, Rein awoke to find Captain Tzatara leaning over the table across from his desk where he focused intently on a large map. It only took her a moment to remember what she had wished to tell him and she jumped to her feet before she had awakened completely.

"Captain!" she called. Captain Tzatara only glanced up from his map at her. "I have a proposition for you about the key."

The captain contemplated for a moment. Then he slowly approached his desk and took a seat where he folded his hands in front of him. "And what might this proposition be?"

"You can meet me at the Springs," Rein offered. "That way, my friend will be able to finish her business with the key and I can get wings again. Then, I will fly over to the Springs to meet you there."

"Well, I don't trust ya to keep yer word, so that won't work."

Captain Tzatara was about to return to his map, but Rein wasn't going to give up so easily. This was the last chance she had.

"Then here's what we can do," she insisted. "I'll give you my word as a fairy that after I get wings, I will meet you at the springs."

"What be so special about yer word as a fairy?" the captain asked. "Ye swore an oath not to disclose any such information, but yer suggesting to do so anyway."

"When we made those oaths, we didn't know that we could bind each other to them to trust the secrets remain what they are. Once we did find out, most of us refused to renew such vows for varieties of different reasons, myself included."

"I see. So how do we bind ya to a vow?"

"There's a bit of fairy magic involved on my part. I announce the oath and we mix each other's blood so that my blood runs through your veins and vice versa. After which, I have no choice but to follow through with my word."

Captain Tzatara stroked his red beard as he contemplated Rein's words. Rein braced herself for his reply.

"So there be no way that ye can break this vow?" the captain asked.

"If I do I die," Rein answered.

"How do I know for a fact that what ya say be true?"

"You'll see it working. If you don't see anything happen when I make the oath, you can break it off and we'll make another deal."

There was a moment of silence while the captain processed the proposition further. Then he stood from his seat to approach his bookcase where he brought out the book of Xyntriav World Wonders. Beads of sweat collected on Rein's forehead, and she wondered if the captain intended to make her finish it like she had offered before. Instead he searched through the pages when he returned to his desk, and then he stopped to read one. Finally, he brought the book up to Rein so she could see the page.

"Is this what ya plan to do?" he asked.

Rein gaped at the words as she read them. Her eyebrows furrowed once she finished. Why would the Fairy Circle add such a weakness to this book? Rein felt a new hatred toward them grow within her, but she forced the feeling away for the time being and addressed the captain.

"Yes," she said.

"Very well," said Captain Tzatara. "I also want yer word that I will enter the Springs."

"I can do that."

"And what happens say, one of us reaches the Cataras Springs before the other?"

"We'll both be bound until the vow is fulfilled," Rein explained. "We'll be able to sense each other to some degree and we can work to arrive at around the same time."

"I can accept that," the captain said. "So how do we do this?"

"You prick your finger and I slit my hand and we mix our blood together," Rein answered. "Pretty simple on your end."

Captain Tzatara removed an ornate, golden knife from a drawer in his desk and pricked his pointer finger to draw some blood. Then he let Rein out of the jar and held the blade of the knife toward her. Rein removed the black glove from her left hand.

"I give you my word as a fairy that after I get wings again, I will meet you at the Cataras Springs and you will enter *if* you give me the detailed location of the Mystery Miracle Worker."

Immediately after she uttered the words, Rein slit her hand on the blade of the knife and the cut ignited with a dim, golden hue. When her blood came into contact with the captain's, a streak of bright gold light shot up both their arms and disappeared.

Rein observed the mahogany scar on her palm which bore a faint gold glow, just like the prick on the captain's finger. He rubbed his thumb and forefinger together and Rein covered her mark with her glove.

"There," said Rein. "Now, if you don't answer my question honestly, with detail, and if I don't obtain wings, the vow terminates itself. So, where do I find the Mystery Miracle Worker?"

Captain Tzatara chuckled as he stood from his seat and returned the book of wonders to his bookcase. "I admire ya, Little Pixie. That was very clever. But it was unnecessary. I be a man of my word."

The captain removed the leather-bound journal and brought it back to his desk.

"You were right that she lives on Roznova," he continued as he unfolded the map in front of Rein. He pointed to a random inkblot. "She lives right there. Though it's not that simple." The captain flipped the map over to reveal more information written in Dovish. "She lives in a cave covered in much green. Once ya actually find the cave, there be three more caves inside, and once ya find the right cave again, her lair be behind a wall. It's gonna take ya a while to find it, so listen carefully.

"The entrance to the first cave looks merely like a hill in the ground. Among the greenery be a willow tree, a glowflower bush, and a cluster of purple rocks. Usually the hill be covered in moss and leafy vines growing from the glowflower bush, so just move all those aside. You will reveal the opening, which be a large rock, but I fancy you'll squeeze yerself in somehow. Once yer inside, go deep into that cave and you'll come up to three other passages. Continue down the one on the far left. Farther inside, there will be a large crease in the wall shaped like a door to your left, but it blends in very well with the rocks, so be sure to look closely. There's a torch hanging next to it, so that on top of knowing what you're looking for should help ya find it. On the other side of that door be the Mystery Miracle Worker's lair."

"Lovely," Rein said clearly not looking forward to this hunt. "I'll need time to memorize all that. I assume you've gotten miracles done by her before?"

"Of course."

"How do you pay?"

"You'll have to figure out methods of payment with her."

"I see." Rein thought for a moment and glanced back at the map. "I need you to take me to Arcor."

Captain Tzatara almost objected, but then he remembered that Rein was wingless. He pursed his lips and then stood from his seat. "I suppose I have no choice."

"You only need to take me close enough so that I can catch a bird to fly the rest of the way there."

The captain shrugged as he approached his cabin doors. "Well that's a little helpful since me first mate won't be too thrilled when I tell him to head back to Arcor."

Chapter Seven

Rein sat atop the tallest mast of the *Blood Omen* for several hours waiting for a bird—any bird—to come within her rope's reach. For the first hour, she didn't mind the wait. It felt grand to finally be out of that cigar case—out of the cabin entirely. Fresh air, even salty sea air, was healing. But at the end of this hour of breathing the odors of fish and low tide, Rein felt like she had enough and enacted the use of the bird calls she had taught herself during the past few centuries without wings. Just when she thought she would lose her voice, a seagull landed about two feet from her. She slowly pushed herself to her feet after learning it couldn't talk and grasped her small rope of twine.

When Rein successfully looped the seagull's beak, the bird took off with her clinging desperately onto the end of the rope. She struggled to climb the twine as swiftly as possible while the seagull glided past the starboard side of the ship and then out to sea. Soon, Rein managed to mount onto the bird's back as it swerved madly to-and-fro. It was a battle, but eventually Rein took complete control of the seagull and flew it to Arcor where she safely landed atop a bell-tower, the tallest building inside the massive, anarchic city.

Rein, still mounted on her feathered ride, scanned the decay that was Arcor City for any sign of Empress Renée, but the city was so massive as it extended to the northern horizon that it was impossible to examine the entire metropolis from where she sat. It didn't help that the many fires spotting the city produced the smoke which further obscured her vision. She began to wonder if the empress had already learned of the location of the Mystery Miracle Worker. Or maybe she got caught with the key and someone had kidnapped her. No—it was too difficult to kidnap a naiad. But perhaps Renée had followed whoever might have stolen the key from her. No—Renée wasn't so bold of a person. If someone had taken the key, the empress would have given up and returned to the ocean. Rein didn't even want to consider that.

Rein tried to put herself into the empress's shoes and considered where she may have gone first in her quest to find the Mystery Miracle Worker. Where could one start in a search to find a merchant who would have such information? Rein wasn't about to attempt to talk to any of these people. She would have to hunt for Empress Renée the old-fashioned way.

Rein steered her bird back to the busy port where she slowly drifted among the dirty, angry people with their boats, ships, and rickety carriages. She realized that she didn't even know exactly what to look for since she couldn't be sure what the empress was wearing. She only knew to look for a woman, most likely wearing a lavish cloak of some sort, and chances were she was by herself keeping away from people as much as possible. Rein longed to ask one of these criminals if they had seen a naiad, but she repeatedly reminded herself that they would all be less than helpful.

Rein spent all day exploring every port of Arcor. As Arcor was a massive island, that was a lot of ports and Rein grew rapidly frustrated with her lack of progress. As the Southern sun made its way to the horizon, Rein finally steered the seagull onto a rooftop among a number of pigeons and other seagulls.

"Do any of you talk?" Rein called. She caught a couple of seagulls trading glances with each other and pointed at them. "I saw that! Listen, I'm not from here, and I'm not looking for trouble. I just have a simple question."

The seagulls hesitated but one finally replied, "What?"

"I'm looking for a naiad."

"On land…?" asked the second seagull with a scoff.

"Yes, I realize that's strange, but I know she's here. We recently learned that an Arcorian merchant knows the location of the Mystery Miracle Worker, so she's looking for him."

"Oh, well I can at least give you that much," said a third seagull and Rein leaned forward in anticipation. "People say that the merchant who owns the Worldly Trade shop learned that information from a pirate. As for your naiad friend, I don't have a clue."

"That's perfect! That may be enough! Can you point me in the direction of this shop?"

The seagulls looked at each other again.

"Sure, it's closer to a southern port," said the second seagull. "Main Port, I think. There's a picture of Xyntriav above his door."

"I think he's right beside a blacksmith… some sort of smith," the first seagull offered. "The merchant's feet are on backwards."

"Wonderful!" Rein praised. "Thank you so much!"

Rein steered the seagull which she rode back to the ports to the south of the island where she began her long search for the Worldly Trade shop. It was just as tedious as her previous search, but Rein was thrilled to finally be on track in some way.

Empress Renée had spent the night in the murky water of the river which coursed through most of Arcor. She had been less than comfortable sleeping in polluted surroundings, but she felt safer there than she would've in any inn the city had to offer. The next day, she felt strangely relieved to exit the river as the Southern and Northern suns leveled out in the sky to mark noon. She carefully made her way back to the barred windows of the Worldly Trade shop where she found the door locked with not only numerous locks, but what seemed to be an Elvic or Farian curse of some kind.

Renée was not pleased to have to stand around in the open Arcor air waiting for this merchant to show up. She pulled the hood of her cloak close around her blonde hair in the hopes of hiding herself from the endless criminal mischief around her, and for a brief moment, she almost longed for the protective walls of the Obsidian Palace. However, her sorrowful memories of feeling hopelessly suffocated and closed off to the outside world ended that potential longing before it had a chance to develop into something more. She quickly concluded that she hated Arcor and the Obsidian Palace equally, only for different reasons.

Eventually, Renée recognized the grimy merchant with his backwards feet approaching his shop with a large leather tube under his arm, and a tall, lanky partner at his side. Renée was relieved to finally have some protective walls around her to separate her from the chaos of the city, but she was wary of the merchant's suspicious second. Neither could approach the door fast enough and their apparent carelessness trod on her patience.

"He arrives at last," Renée deadpanned.

"I did say noon," said the merchant. "If you've been waiting long, that is no fault of mine."

Renée didn't bother arguing with the man, afraid that it would slow him down further as he took his time unlocking the many locks on his rotting door. Finally, he stepped inside and Renée quickly moved to follow him, only to be stopped by the silver force-field which remained guarding the threshold.

"Patience, my Lady," said the merchant. He fiddled with something which Renée couldn't see and the silver shimmer faded. "Now you may enter."

Renée obeyed without response. The partner trailed behind and locked the door while Renée continued to follow the merchant to a large desk at the very back of his cluttered shop. She watched him remove a large sheet of rolled up parchment from the leather tube.

"You brought the key, I hope," he said as he flattened the sheet on his desk.

Renée only answered by lifting the key from her light blue bodice, but left it hanging around her neck. The merchant glanced at her while he set weights on the corners of the parchment and Renée kept a watchful eye on the partner, who now approached the desk to stand with them. After catching her leering at him, the partner made sure to keep his distance.

Finally, the merchant stood up straight and gestured to the sheet on his desk. "This is a map of Roznova."

"One of the Continent Islands," Renée confirmed.

"Exactly." The merchant pointed to a spot on the map; the same spot Captain Tzatara had shown Rein. "This red dot is where the Mystery Miracle Worker is located."

Clearly Renée wasn't satisfied with this snippet of information. "Is that below ground, in a cave, up a tree…?"

"Beneath a hill covered in moss and glowflower bushes," the merchant responded. "But see, beneath this hill is in fact, three separate passages. Be sure you take the left one. Then there's a door hidden in the wall beside a torch. She'll be behind that door."

"Beneath a hill through the wall of the cave to the left." Renée leaned over the desk to gather a better glimpse at the red dot on the map. "Anything else I should know?"

"I hope you have something practical to trade because she doesn't accept currency as payment."

Renée stood up straight. "Duly noted. Thank you for your time."

"The key, if you will," said the merchant before Renée turned to leave. He held out his hand. "We did have a deal after all."

Renée brushed the key with her white, delicate fingers and giggled. "Oh, you mean this eroded antique..."

Suddenly, Renée melted to the ground right before the eyes of the merchant and his partner, and coursed out of the shop with the key. The two men cried out in panic and chased after her, nearly breaking down the door as they exited. They whipped their heads left and right along the ground in desperate search for the naiad.

"There! Right there!" the merchant's partner pointed.

"Ready your knife," the merchant snarled as he stormed toward the moving pool of water.

The merchant seized a piece of trashed plywood off the ground as his partner drew his knife and followed closely after him. When the merchant caught up to the living water, he rammed the plywood in the ground in front of it so that it crashed into the barricade. The water formed back into the figure of Empress Renée, who wore a dazed expression on her face. Here, the partner slashed at the empress with his knife, but he may as well have slashed at a phantom. He succeeded in snatching her attention though, so that the merchant had the perfect opportunity to rip the key from her neck. Renée attempted to snatch it back only to be socked in the face. She took the merchant and his partner by surprise when the punch had the same effect as a punch to a puddle. Water splashed from her head and returned to her feet as her face quickly recovered before the men's eyes. The merchant shook his head in disbelief and his partner had to grab in him by the arm to get him to run away with the key.

Empress Renée collapsed at the base of a tree with a sad, squishy plop, and she held her face where she had been hit. Then she watched the merchant and his partner run off with the key… her key… her only hope of ever finding joy, healing, bearing children… and saving her adopted daughter's life. Her eyes welled up with tears and her nose gleamed red as she let it all sink in. After finally coming to terms with her failure, Renée sobbed uncontrollably for a considerable period of time, like a small child with her knees to her chin.

"Renée! Renée, get up! Get up!"

The voice sounded familiar to the empress. She craned her head to gaze up into the tree where she caught sight of her old pixie friend.

"Rein? What are you doing here?"

"I came to join you in finding the Mystery Miracle Worker," Rein answered as she set her feathered ride free.

"I lost the key, Rein," the empress replied with more tears in her voice.

"I saw that, but I found where they took it. I'll need your help getting it back though. You want to get it back, right?" The empress nodded. "Great, I'll show you the way."

Rein climbed down the tree and hopped onto the empress's shoulders, then she pointed at a section of the forest line. The empress wiped her face, pushed her shoulders back, and marched into the forest where Rein directed.

Out of the sight of the pixie and the empress, a mysterious man dressed in a silver cloak had watched the whole spectacle from behind an abandoned bakery. He kept his face hidden with the shadow of his hood and had the presence of a wanderer, yet he carried little on him. He was careful not to be seen before he emerged from his hiding spot. Only he knew of his intentions as he followed the two girls. It seemed as though they may be of some use to him.

Rein led the empress along a river deeper through the thick trees. Here the air was much cleaner and the aura much calmer. The river thinned out into a creek and they followed it into the mouth of a cave where the temperature grew colder. The creek led them to the back of the cave where it disappeared beneath the wall.

"There's a door there somewhere," Rein explained. "I think we can both slip underneath though."

Without a word in reply, the empress melted into a puddle again and did exactly as Rein suggested. Meanwhile, Rein discovered a tiny hole through which she barely managed to fit. On the other side, Rein spotted a set of stair-steps carved into the rock. They led down into a steep cavity where they disappeared into darkness. The trickling of the tiny waterfall echoed up this stairwell, the hollow shape of which amplified the sound. Carefully, Rein made her way down each of the slippery steps, but they were wet and mossy and she slipped. She clawed desperately at her rocky surroundings to gain purchase, but everything was too damp to grab a firm hold and she continued to fall into the darkness with a yelp. Thankfully, the empress heard Rein's cry and managed to catch the pixie before she collided with the rocky floor.

"Thank you," Rein breathed, and the empress set her back on her shoulder. Then they both turned around and stood aghast once they realized where they were: expanding before them was an enormous rock city with no evident city-folk. The lair was dark but full of vegetation, and the tiny creek appeared to continue through to the other end of this city. The air was musty but filled with floral perfume. The only source of light was the torches that lined the ghost town where every single building was made of some form of stone. Some homes were even carved into the walls.

As empty as the realm seemed to be, Renée was awestruck by its beauty. There were trees and gardens everywhere, crops to keep the missing residents alive, and flowers which added more color to the lawns and gray domiciles. There were even some livestock, all which were white or gray in color. Far out in the distance, she made out a large, white castle on a cliff top, also decorated in vibrant plant-life. Its glistening spires reached up to the cave's ceiling while the structure teetered over the abyss below. There were signs of life everywhere the girls looked. There had to be people somewhere, but where could they all be?

The empress entered the city with her fairy friend on her shoulder, and they continued to use the creek as their guide as it flowed down the center of the limestone streets. They soon found that they advanced down the main road which led all the way to the castle, and they proceeded down this road with vigilance in search of either of the two men who took the key.

It was here when the mysterious man descended the stairs and peered into the city himself. He remained stationary and watched the two girls with hidden eyes. Rein and Renée kept watch for any signs of people, but by the time they had reached the center of the city, they were ready to confirm that they were the only life forms around.

Suddenly, there resounded a loud BOOM! The empress hid in the creek while Rein sprinted to the closest torch and scrambled up near the flame so that the firelight would hide her glow. The mysterious man stepped back into the shadows of the stairwell. They all stared in the direction that the noise had come from and waited in anxious silence to discover the cause.

Chapter Eight

The silence which followed the thundering burst seemed to last for hours and the three trespassers almost decided to continue forward until they heard emphatic, synchronized marching. The footsteps echoed about the lair and grew fuller, louder, as though they increased in numbers. The girls and the mysterious man watched from their hiding spots as they finally caught sight of an army dressed in white and gray, slowly marching toward them. This army was made up of both men and women, and it was larger than any army any of them had ever seen. The soldiers were separated into groups, each turning down individual streets until every gap in the city, every alley and corner was occupied. Then all at once they stopped marching and for a moment all was eerily silent. Then followed the chant of a deep male's voice as it echoed about the realm, giving the soldiers orders, forcing them to rehearse.

If these people have the key, Xyntriav is doomed, Rein thought. Now she had a new reason to retrieve the key besides surviving her oath to Captain Tzatara, and she felt the urge swell within her to do so as soon as possible. She glanced at the palm of her left hand—the mark of her promise itched beneath her glove. Rein pulled her coat tightly around her to hide as much of her own natural light as possible and jumped from the lamppost to a small tree. She ripped one of the leaves from the branches and then scurried down to the ground where she whispered into the creek.

"If those two men have anything to do with this, we can't let them keep the key."

Renée's head slowly emerged from the surface of the water. "No," she breathed.

Though the empress fully agreed with Rein, these individuals with their hooded robes made her skin crawl with a strange mix of fear and loathing. She glanced back toward the stairwell from which she came and fought the desire to turn back.

"My guess is they brought the key to their ruler," Rein continued.

"You think we should search the castle?" Renée asked.

"I think that's our best bet, and I think that this creek will lead us there." Rein set the leaf on the ground next to the creek and hopped on top of it. "You can flow there with the current and I can float with you on this leaf."

"I hope this is wise," said the empress as she pulled the leaf into the creek.

Together, the empress and the pixie coursed along with the creek toward the White Castle, which they soon understood was from where the soldiers had emerged. Meanwhile, the mysterious man stayed behind and watched the tiny leaf float deeper into the city while he calculated his next move.

The creek proceeded to flow under the massive platinum doors to the castle, and since Empress Renée and Rein were able to fit beneath them, they entered the structure easily. They both took a moment to glance around at the grand foyer when they emerged. The castle had been carved from whitestone and must have taken decades to forge. Whoever ruled this underground world had bright and colorful taste to say the least. The residents of this fortress practically lived in an enormous garden complete with birds, butterflies, and shapely marble statues. There was even a large koi pond by the fireplace in the grand sitting room. Neither the empress nor Rein were impressed with these surroundings. While it reminded the empress of her sorry courtyard behind the Obsidian Palace, it reminded Rein of the Maja Forest.

"What makes you think this is where they took the key?" Renée whispered.

"Because clearly these people are brainwashed by some higher power," Rein answered. "It's a cult. The Arcorians would have taken the key to their leader rather than keep it for themselves. And where else can this leader live besides the only castle here?"

"Do you have an idea as to where it would be?"

"Not a clue. Perhaps the leader's chamber or study… Of course, I don't know where either are located."

Empress Renée scanned her bright and massive surroundings once more. Her anxiety only increased with each passing moment and she was eager to leave this eerie lair. "Well then we best begin our search."

"Fine. You search the level above us, I'll stay down here," Rein suggested. "Don't get caught."

The empress exited the creek and quickly ascended the marble steps of the stairwell while Rein roamed the lawn on the first level. The pixie remained vigilant against the birds which resided in this indoor garden. Though she was capable of rounding them up and riding them, many were still predators to her and she was especially vulnerable without wings. After running about the tall grass and dodging the butterflies, Rein finally found what she assumed to be the study. She sprinted inside and decided she would explore the pewter desk first. She climbed to the top and searched in all the boxes and around all the knickknacks only to come up empty-handed, at which point she plopped down on the desk to rest. This was going to be a long night for her and the empress.

Suddenly there was that familiar BOOM that she and Renée had heard earlier, only this time it was closer and louder, just down the corridor. Rein jumped down from the desk and dashed over to the window seat where she hid beneath the white, pegasus-feather blanket that had been neatly laid out on top of the light blue cushion.

Outside the study, Rein overheard a conversation between two male voices and she wondered, *What happened to the army? Didn't they come from inside this castle?* She lost this thought when she noticed that the voices grew rapidly closer until they eventually entered the study.

"It just needs to be larger and undoubtedly unstoppable!" said the first voice.

"Yes, sire," replied the second. "And now we have help for that."

"Yes, but the key won't do us much good until we learn where to find the Springs."

Rein carefully lifted one of the pegasus feathers so that she could observe the two gentlemen. The larger man took a seat behind the pewter desk while the taller, lankier one took a seat in front of it.

"Well, Lazar says he knows someone who can help us with that too," said the lanky man.

"Yes, you keep telling me that, Cloid. But I don't trust seadogs."

"It's worth a shot though, Your Excellency," Cloid insisted. "Don't you think?"

The leader sighed and narrowed his eyes at Cloid, unconvinced for the most part. "If you insist," he finally said, defeated. "Send him in."

"Before I do that, sire, do you think we should hide the key somewhere else rather than the k—"

"*Cloid!* The only way anyone will know its location is if you don't keep your blinkin' mouth shut!"

"Yes, sire. My apologies. I'll send in Lazar."

Cloid left for only a moment and returned with a third man whom Rein recognized as the abarimon merchant. Then it dawned on her that she recognized Cloid to be the merchant's partner. It seemed that not only had these two pledged their loyalties to this leader, they worked directly beneath him as well. Rein continued to watch as the merchant, Lazar, bowed to the leader who nodded his head in return.

"Lazar," said Cloid. "It is my honor to introduce you to His Excellency, Grand Master Jaska Astig."

"It's an honor, Your Excellency," Lazar said.

"Have a seat, Lazar," Jaska replied as he gestured to one of the chairs in front of his desk.

Rein sighed quietly and rolled her eyes as it appeared that these men were beginning a meeting. She had no choice but to remain where she was until it was finished. She could only hope that it wouldn't be long.

"My advisor here tells me you claim to know someone who can tell us where the Cataras Springs are," Jaska continued.

"Yes, Your Excellency," Lazar replied.

"Well go on then," Jaska urged. "Tell me who this person is."

"Just like that?" Lazar asked with a glance to Cloid. "No offering of anything?"

"I already paid you for the key," said Jaska.

"And now you're asking for information. I would like something else in return."

"How about I promise that I won't beat it out of you?" Jaska snarled. "How does that sound?"

"I want something in return for the information, though," Lazar pressed, unfazed by the threat.

"What exactly would you like, Seadog?"

"I would like to reside in this lovely palace you have here."

"You have to work in the palace to live in it, fool!"

"Well then give me a job."

Jaska paused. "What can you do?"

"Well I am a merchant, after all. I can bring supplies, recruit more soldiers for your army, find another hiding spot when this place becomes too small, add more members to your infamous league, and run other errands."

Jaska appeared to consider for a long moment. "Very well," he finally resolved. "Cloid will train you on the rules and regulations of the palace. Now, tell me who can help us."

"The Mystery Miracle Worker," said Lazar simply.

Jaska was taken aback. "And I assume you know where the Mystery Miracle Worker lives?"

"Yes, Your Excellency. But that's a whole other issue. We'll need to make another deal."

Jaska threw himself over the desk and snatched Lazar by the collar. "I'm not in the mood to play games, *Seadog*! You will tell me where she lives, or as I said before, I will beat it out of you!"

"On Roznova!" Lazar blurted out. "I'd have to show you in person though! It's difficult to explain the whereabouts of her lair with mere words."

"You can't draw me a picture or show me on a map of Roznova?" Jaska growled as he threw Lazar back into his seat.

"No, sire. It's too complicated."

Jaska sat in thought for another moment. "Take him to his new room, Cloid. I have some thinking to do."

"Yes, Your Excellency," said Cloid, who then turned to Lazar. "Follow me."

Rein was stunned. In a matter of two days she had found three people who knew the location of the Mystery Miracle Worker, including this leader who would soon learn. If Cloid also learned, that would make four. It wouldn't be much longer before this poor woman would have to find a new hiding place.

At this point, Empress Renée had scrutinized every option the second level had to offer and got nowhere. She felt as though it had taken her until the next morning to complete her investigation, and having nothing to show for it made her want to toss every potted plant she passed against the blindingly immaculate white walls. She brought her rage under control as she stormed back to the staircase which led to the first floor and began to wonder how Rein was doing in her search. When she heard footsteps coming up the marble stairs, the empress melted and coursed the rest of the way down, passing the two men who ascended up the stairs, then flowed back into the creek. There the empress hid and slowly poked her head through the surface of the water to scan the area for Rein. The pixie was nowhere to be found.

"Rein?" the empress whispered. "Rein! Rein?"

In the study, Jaska lifted his head from his paperwork at the sound of someone calling for a stranger by the name of Rein. This was Rein's chance to escape while he was presently distracted. She wrapped herself in her coat as best she could under the feathered blanket. Jaska pushed himself up from his desk and approached the door to open it, at which point Rein sprinted from behind him and ran out to hide beneath a table beside the study. She paused and peered up at Jaska as he glanced around for the source of the voice he had heard. Rein released the breath she held when she confirmed she had successfully gone unnoticed.

Empress Renée submerged herself completely in the creek when she saw the door to the study open. She kept quiet and listened for the door to close before she believed it was safe to resurface. It felt like forever until she heard the subtle sound of the door shutting, and cautiously she emerged from the creek. She spotted Rein climbing to the top of the side-table.

"Did you find it?" Renée whispered.

"No," Rein answered. "I haven't had the chance to search everywhere down here, I got stuck in the study. We'll just have to keep looking. You try the third floor, I'll continue down here."

The empress heaved a frustrated sigh. "Very well."

Rein took a seat where she stood and racked her brain for a long moment. Cloid was about to say where the key was, but of course Jaska had interrupted him. However, the first letter sound he made of "k" narrowed down the choices significantly. Rein pondered all the possible places the key could be located which started with that sound: key holder, kitchen, cocktail bar, kindling. All these things were possible but she didn't know where most of them were located… except for the kindling. Rein scurried to the fireplace and searched among the firewood with her adrenaline rushing and her excitement growing ever stronger. It all went up in smoke when she still didn't find the key.

Meanwhile, Empress Renée glided swiftly up the stairwell to the third level of the White Castle where she paused to assess her surroundings. She glanced up and down the large corridor without a clue as to where to go from there. This level appeared to be the floor where Jaska would board his guests as there were significantly more rooms than the second level. The second level had been more spacious with the rooms more open, and seemed to be the floor where meetings were held and guests were entertained, therefore making it easier to search. But on the third level, every single room was behind a closed door, and there were many, many rooms.

Renée fell against the wall, defeated. There were so many doors, most likely each with hundreds of places to hide a key beyond them, and she would have to search them *all.* In that moment, she would have given anything to avoid this grand exploration and leave the underground lair. But no, she had to make it to the Cataras Springs and drink from the Spring of Healing. She also had to make it appear as though she was trying to save Nadia so that she could regain the empire's favor. Even though Nadia wasn't actually *her* daughter, it would look bad to the empire if she gave up simply because she didn't want to search through a handful of bedchambers. So with a heavy sigh, she melted and slipped beneath the door to the first chamber.

Back on the bottom level, Rein scanned the sitting room and tried to think of where the kitchen could possibly be until she spotted the koi pond. Of course! The koi pond! She cautiously crept up to the pool and peered into the bright blue water. Sure enough, the key was at the bottom… amid the fish. Fish were among the worst predators for pixies and sprite creatures as they were more difficult to dodge when one was trapped in their habitat. Rein rubbed her face. She would have to go for it if she were to retrieve the key before the empress could. She couldn't trust Renée with it anymore, though it was easy for the empress to take it away from her. She'd have to figure out a way to keep it from the empress while still allowing her to know how much time she had left. But first and foremost, Rein needed to retrieve the key.

Rein removed her coat and satchel of burdania petals while she whispered a quick prayer. Then, against her better judgement, she dove in. The sudden splash startled the fish for a moment, which allowed Rein enough time to reach the key without interference. She tugged vigorously on the key, but it was stubbornly stuck among the rocks and dirt at the bottom of the pond. Slowly the fish started to drift toward Rein, and she felt it necessary to swim back to the surface and exit before they decided to nibble at her.

Rein sat next to the water soaking wet and watched the koi go back to their mindless swimming routine as she considered how to get that key out safely. She might be able to use the chain as leverage. After a moment to collect her courage, Rein dove back in, snatched the chain, and climbed back out before the fish had a chance to react. That was when she found that the chain was broken and she had separated it from the key. Rein whipped the chain against the whitestone floor with a frustrated growl, then rubbed her face to try and calm down. Everything that could go wrong…

By this time, the fish were waiting and ready for Rein's next attempt to fetch the key. The only solution she could come up with was to use her sword from Captain Tzatara to fight them away. Then, she would thread the chain through the loop on the key, bring the chain back out of the water, and pull the key out. Yes, this was the plan. Yes, it would work.

Rein waited a little while longer for the koi to perhaps give up while she ran her plan over and over in her head. Then, after psyching herself up one last time, she dove back into the pond, looped the loop, and jumped back out. For a moment, Rein relished in the relief of victory until something latched onto her left leg and she felt herself being dragged back into the water. Rein hardly had the chance to refill her lungs with fresh air before she was submerged. She desperately kicked the koi with her right foot, but the fish was too hungry to let go. Soon Rein spotted a couple of his pals swimming her way and she fought not to gasp. Then she remembered her sword. As she continued to use her free leg to push away from the scaly beast, she drew her sword and stabbed the fish in the head with it. To her despair, the infliction did nothing besides draw a couple drops of blood. She had to exact another wound in the fish's eye before it finally released her leg and she kicked herself back to the surface, barely avoiding the jaws of his hungry buddies.

Rein checked the wounds she received from the koi's tiny teeth and found them to be minor flesh wounds, which only appeared serious due to the blood drawn. She would heal, although walking and running would be significantly more strenuous. Rein slowly brought herself back to her feet and began to pull on the chain to get the key out of the mud at the bottom of the pond. Once it finally came loose, the force of the release caused Rein to fall backward. She didn't bother to stand back up as she gently fished the key out of the water, being careful not to make too much noise.

"Oh! You found it!" came the empress who forgot to be quiet.

The sudden exclamation caused Rein to flinch as her nerves were still shot from her recent near-death experience. She turned to see Empress Renée rushing into the sitting room, her blue dress swaying like disturbed water around her. She hurried up to Rein and seized the key into her hands. Rein knew there was nothing that she could do to keep the key from the empress, so she just sheathed her sword, replaced her jacket, and swung her satchel over her shoulder without a word.

"We haven't much time," said the empress as she tied the chain around her neck. "We must go now!"

Before Rein could reply, the empress snatched her up and turned to find Jaska stepping out of his study to observe what all the yelling was about.

Chapter Nine

Jaska observed Empress Renée who held the precious key in her right hand and a glowing sprite creature in her other. A fiendish smirk stretched across his face. They had been caught and Rein wished that the empress would do something besides just stand there in stark terror. If she would at least release Rein...

"Cloid!" Jaska called.

The empress melted and surged into the creek, leaving Rein to fend for herself. The poor pixie, heavy from still being drenched, darted beneath a table as fast as she could with her wounded leg. Cloid and Lazar had exited the study right as the empress took refuge. Immediately Lazar grabbed an empty vase from a side table and scooped her up from the stream. Keeping her inside the vase was a tricky feat, but Cloid managed to plug the opening shut with a clay pot. They thought the fight would be over at that point, but the naiad continued to leak through the gaps between the pot and the vase.

Meanwhile, Jaska went after Rein who desperately searched for a mouse hole of some sort, but found nothing. Jaska repeatedly lunged at her, nearly pouncing on her, desperately trying to catch her and in doing so, made a mess of his palace foyer.

"Rein!" cried the empress as she fought to escape the vase.

Rein's attention snapped to the cry for help and she paused to look in Renée's direction. This gave Jaska the perfect opportunity to snatch her up. He held her tightly with her hands at her sides so she didn't have access to her sword or dagger. The three men took a moment to catch their breath once the scuffle had ended. Jaska addressed Lazar and Cloid.

"Follow me."

Jaska took Rein up the stairs while Cloid and Lazar followed, carrying the empress in the vase. He led them all up five stories to a large, gray room, where the walls were bloodstained and riddled with chains and bolts. On a table to the left Rein observed a number of random objects such as a large porcelain bowl, dead critters, a broken carriage wheel, silverware, whips, and a large birdcage. Jaska locked Rein in the birdcage and hung it from a chain hooked to the tall ceiling. Then he addressed his servants.

"Toss her in there." He gestured to a concrete box. "And grab the key while you're at it."

Lazar unlocked the chain which held the coffer shut and with Cloid's help, lifted the heavy lid to reveal an assortment of strange and disturbing torture devices. As Cloid poured the empress into this frightening trunk of horrors, Lazar reached to grab the key. To Rein's surprise, the empress managed to shoot water down Lazar's windpipe, but the lid was brought down on her before she could finish suffocating him. The bit of water in Lazar's throat rushed back in with the rest of Renée just before they tightly locked the lid with a chain and padlock, but Rein had a new respect for the empress. She didn't know Renée had it in her to fight back.

Cloid took a seat on the box while Lazar squat in front of him, both taking another moment to catch their breath. Pride swelled in Rein. At least she and the empress had made these men work hard for their capture.

"All right," Jaska breathed. "Give me the key and let's go."

Lazar obeyed and together they left the room, locking the door behind them. Rein examined the windowless door to this dull yet horrific room, and she promptly surmised that there was not enough space beneath the door for her to simply slip out. She glanced around and while there were no rodent holes in these walls, she spotted a barred window near the ceiling. She knew she could easily get out of that cage, she would just have to figure out how to get to that window. She continued to scrutinize her prison and learned that there was no rope, no shelves, not enough bolts sticking out of the walls that would help her climb to the window. There weren't even enough cracks and holes; the entire castle was so aggravatingly pristine! So, Rein's next thought was to wait behind the door for the Jaska or his servants to return, and she could sneak out that way.

There was no doubt in Rein's mind that they would return, and most likely soon. If they hadn't figured out she was a pixie yet, they would certainly come back to interrogate her about her ethnicity. Upon learning that she's a pixie it would immediately follow that Rein could answer all their questions regarding the Cataras Springs. Yes, they would return, and very soon.

Gravity on Xyntriav was a lot lighter than on Earth, so one was able to jump or fall from taller heights without the risk of death or injury. However, the fall from the birdcage Rein had been locked in was especially far, and Rein wasn't sure she could trust it, especially with her leg injury. So she thought to make the cage swing on its chain, and then she would launch herself to the table against the wall.

The cage was so large, and the chain long and heavy that it was a slow and grueling process dashing back and forth inside it. Her injured leg soon ached from the tireless running, but the swinging was effective and Rein knew that if she just kept working a little longer, she could get the cage to swing a little farther. She grasped the bar after a lap and peered down at the table, then ran back to the other side of the cage. This was it. Rein sprinted once again across the bottom of the birdcage and then launched herself from it.

Almost immediately, Rein knew that she would make her target. She soared through the air and when she touched down she tucked and rolled across the table, landing among the rotting rats, squirrels, and the chipmunk. The maneuver may have avoided a fracture, but it did little to prevent pain and her ending location failed to offer any comfort. She scrambled away from the furry corpses, then cradled her injured leg and waited for the awful throbbing to subside.

When the pain had faded enough to bear, Rein made haste to the stone trunk inside which the empress was held. Hot with adrenaline, she scaled the chain to reach the pad lock. There she examined the lock and though she knew it was hopeless, she removed her glove and coat and tried to stretch her hand inside the mechanism anyway. The sharp metal scratched against her skin and she made more progress than she thought she would, but she failed to reach far enough to fiddle with the components. Even though Rein had made a fair effort, she felt like she hadn't spent enough time trying to unlock the latch to justify giving up. Maybe she could force her arm farther into the lock. She willed her arm to be thinner, relaxed her muscles, and clenched her teeth as she rammed her arm deeper into the apparatus.

A sharp pang shot up to Rein's shoulder and lingered on her forearm, but her heart skipped as she felt the lock's mechanism at the tips of her fingers. If she could just press through the pain a little longer, she could free the empress and they could escape together. Rein breathed a few soothing breaths to fuel her endurance before she gave her arm one last shove that aggravated the fresh cut. She whimpered against a bit lip and her heart dropped when she made no progress. She panted in pain and dropped her head against the padlock as she came to terms with the fact that she was going to need the key.

Rein braced herself before she yanked her arm out of the lock with a strained groan and examined the large bloody gash that resulted. She glanced around for something to use to stopper the wound, but there was only her coat, still wet from her dive in the koi pond. She hated it, but all she could do was put the coat back on and let the sleeve act as a bandage on its own. That was when she heard footsteps coming down the hallway beyond the door, along with the familiar voices of Lazar and Cloid.

"I'll figure out how to get us out of here, Renée," she said as she shrugged the coat back on. "Hang tight."

With that, Rein rapidly approached the door and stood aside to wait for their captors to open it. The moment Jaska's servants entered, Rein snuck out before they noticed she was no longer in the birdcage. She gnashed her teeth against the burning ache in her arm as she scurried up the side of a chair which sat against a wall. The pain increased as she pulled herself up the side of the picture frame hanging above the chair, and climbed onto the sconce of an oil lamp so that her light would blend in with the light of the flame. She pulled her cold coat tightly around her to hide her figure and waited for Jaska's servants to exit the room.

"Where'd it go?" came Lazar's voice.

"How did it get out?" came the voice of Cloid.

"I don't know."

"His Excellency isn't going to be pleased."

"What are you going to tell him?" Lazar asked.

"I'm not telling him anything. You tell him. He can't kill you."

"What?" Lazar sounded confused.

"You've got valuable information! He can't kill you unless he's willing to give that information up."

"Why would he kill me in the first place? It's not like I lost the sprite."

"You obviously don't know the Grand Master very well. Anyway, there's nothing to worry about. Like I said, as long as he wants the information you have, he can't kill you."

There was a moment of silence before Lazar said, "Very well. I'll just tell him it escaped on its own."

"Works for me. I'll just wait outside while you tell him."

They left the room in no hurry. Rein, too, was in no hurry to get down from the oil lamp since she wasn't aware of anywhere else she could go. She was also wet, exhausted, achy, and bleeding. If it wasn't so difficult to balance, she would have no qualms with simply falling asleep where she was. Granted it wasn't the wisest option anyway, so she felt she had no choice but to find a safer spot, preferably in accordance with her next mission.

What was Rein's next mission? She had to find a way to free Renée, but it had dawned on her that the lid was too heavy for her to open even if she had unlocked it for the empress. Considering the fact that it was difficult for Lazar to lift it himself since he had required Cloid's help, she imagined that Renée would also have trouble with it. Perhaps it was best to wait until someone let the empress out for whatever purpose it would serve.

Meanwhile, Rein could search for the key and steal it back. She leaned her forehead against the sconce, defeated at the thought alone. She had just spent a couple hours searching for that thing and found it. Now she had to begin her search all over again because obviously Jaska would pick a new hiding spot.

Rein rubbed her face long and hard. She had spent enough time resting and plotting on the sconce; she really needed to find a place to camp out, but as far as she could tell this castle was completely devoid of rodents and their homes. She concluded that she would have to create one herself.

Rein glanced at the picture frame she had used to climb to the sconce and noticed that hung on the wall by nails. She could use a nail to dig herself a place to stay in the wall. She summoned an ounce of energy, jumped onto the top of the picture, and found the nail of her choice. She grasped it with her life and scooted herself between the picture and the wall. As she hung there, she used her feet to yank the nail from the white stone, ignoring the alarming spike of pain which shot up her wounded arm and throbbed in her leg. When she finally got the nail free, the frame swung sideways and Rein managed to snag the corner to keep herself from tumbling helplessly to the floor. Once the swinging had settled, Rein dropped to the cushion of the silver seat below. She crawled beneath the chair and listened for someone to rush over to see what the all the commotion was and who had caused it. No one came, but sitting motionless felt like Heaven to the exhausted pixie.

She set the nail on her lap for a moment and leaned her head back. She had time, she told herself. She deserved a break.

Lazar and Cloid stood outside the bathhouse where they waited for their Grand Master to finish bathing before telling him the disturbing news. The steamy air which filled the corridor was tense and neither of them spoke a word. At long last, the large Grand Master stepped out dressed in a white robe. He chuckled along with the two shapely elves who hung on his arms dressed in flowy matching attire. He stopped at the sight of Cloid and Lazar and furrowed his eyebrows at them.

"Is something wrong?" he asked.

Cloid nudged Lazar and startled him into speaking. "Yes, Your Excellency."

Jaska addressed the elves. "Meet me in the courtyard, ladies."

"Yes, Your Excellency," they answered softly. They curtsied before they glided down the corridor arm-in-arm and Jaska faced his servants.

"Walk and talk, gentlemen."

Cloid and Lazar obeyed while Jaska led them to his chambers.

"Well, to get straight to the point, Your Excellency," Lazar began, "the sprite is missing."

Jaska stopped suddenly and leered at Lazar. "What? How is that possible?"

Lazar shrugged. "She escaped somehow."

Jaska growled and continued to approach his chambers with a heavier step. "And what of the naiad?"

"She remains locked in the chest, Your Excellency," Cloid answered before Lazar had the chance.

"Good," Jaska replied as they entered through a pair of large, platinum doors. He picked up a silver comb from his dresser and combed his hair in front of a large, silver-framed mirror. "She's my main concern. There's no way the sprite can free the naiad, so we'll just keep her there until I come up with something to do with her."

Jaska paused to think and set the comb aside. Cloid swallowed hard and shifted his weight to his other foot. His evident anxiety put Lazar on edge, but Jaska simply lifted the lid off a silver dish to smear a scented cream on his chest. The room suddenly filled with an aroma of magnolia blossoms and finally Jaska shared his thoughts with his servants.

"Let's see, Martalitas is next month. I'll use her for that. In the meantime, let's go see if we can figure out how the sprite escaped. Wait for me outside while I get dressed."

"Yes, Your Excellency," the servants said. They bowed and then exited the room.

By the time the servants and their Grand Master returned to investigate the gray room in the tower, Rein had finished a long, revitalizing nap. The voices of these men brought her to full consciousness and she quickly rushed behind a large mirrored vase farther down the hallway. The conversation ended as soon as they reached the door and the three of them walked inside.

"Good," Rein heard Jaska say moments later. "She's still there. But I can't see how the sprite could've gotten free."

"Well, clearly she could've escaped the birdcage," Lazar said.

"Obviously, you fool!" Jaska exclaimed. "Ever thought that was why I hung the cage by that chain? That still doesn't explain how she got out of the room."

"Maybe she escaped through that window."

"How?"

Lazar couldn't answer.

"Think she's a threat, sire?" came Cloid's voice.

"I doubt it," Jaska said, calmer this time. "Right now, she's the least of my worries. All we have to do is make sure the key *cannot* be found. No doubt that sprite is searching for it. Anyway, I have an army to build, and Martalitas to plan for next month." Rein watched the prison door close after Jaska and his servants exited. "The naiad will be our Facio Ritus."

"How do you plan to kill a naiad?" Cloid asked as they walked away.

"Oh it's simple, and everyone will learn next month during the sacrifice."

Chapter Ten

Rein processed the conversation she had overheard and hundreds of questions ran through her mind: What was Martalitas? What was a Facio Ritus? How could Rein find out? When did they plan to kill Renée and how? Rein tried to shake the questions from her head. From what she had just heard, she would be there for another month, so she should get as comfortable as possible since there were still thirty days left in the month. There would be plenty of time to answer these questions later.

By the time everyone else in the White Castle had gone to bed, Rein had found the optimal spot to create her hiding place in a wall behind a cupboard in the grand kitchen. Before she used the nail to carve out her alcove, she made her way to the bathhouse so that she could wash the blood and fishy odor from her body and clothes. While her clothes dried, she found a stash of thin linens which the Grand Master would use to soak his face, and she tore off some pieces to use as bandages for the wounds on her arm and leg. After finally getting redressed, Rein spotted a basket of potpourri on a countertop and decided this would be her bed. She stopped by a guest room to cut a swab from a blanket for herself as she dragged the basket down the corridor and then finally made her way back to the grand kitchen.

Rein spent many hours chiseling into the wall behind the cupboard—a task which took longer than it would have if she'd had two healthy arms. She eventually paused to rest and realized it may have been wiser to bathe after she had completed this job. She sweat profusely and quickly found herself covered in white dust. Too late now. She brushed the dust off, took a sip of water from a thimble she had set aside for herself, then continued to cut into the wall. Once she was finally finished, she hauled her potpourri bed into the hole, collapsed on top of it, and passed out.

When Rein awoke the next day to the sound of the kitchen staff hastily preparing an upcoming meal, she realized she had absolutely no idea what time it was. She lay in her leafy bed and listened in on the conversations beyond her sanctuary in search of words such as breakfast, brunch, luncheon, or lunch, which one would expect to hear from kitchen staff. For whatever reason, they failed in this regard, and this put Rein in a mood in which few prefer to begin a new day. She continued to eaves-drop as she stretched her sore body, and nibbled on some bread and burdania petals. Her burdania petals… did she have enough to last her a month?

Rein endeavored to remain calm as she dumped the petals and seeds on the floor of her nook and counted. Fifty-four petals, not counting the one she was eating at the time. She contemplated. Rein had planned to use some of these petals as a trade-off for the Mystery Miracle Worker in case the seeds weren't enough. Granted she only planned to stay at the White Castle for another thirty days, but she felt the need to be prepared to stay longer if she ran into more hurdles. This provided her with an extra twenty or so petals and she was required to eat one a day to stay alive without her wings. Could she survive on one every other day? Or perhaps half a petal a day? She couldn't imagine that she would die overnight after skipping one petal.

Rein stuffed the petals and seeds back into her pouch and decided that she would eat this one petal today. Tomorrow, she would learn what would happen if she skipped a day. She had to confess that she looked forward to skipping a day as the burdania flower had a nasty taste. Meanwhile, her next mission was to learn everything she could about Martalitas and Facio Ritus. This seemed necessary if she was going to save Renée. Hopefully, she'd find a clue about the key in the process. Rein remembered there being a bookcase in Jaska's study. Chances were, she might find information on Martalitas in there.

With extreme caution, Rein exited her little hole and peered around the cupboard to assess the situation beyond. There were a couple members of the kitchen staff still rummaging about, but Rein felt it possible for her to avoid their gaze as she zig-zagged around tables, chairs, and counters. Then there were the stairs which led up to the first floor of the castle. They were a completely open, no-man's land, and Rein felt certain that she would be spotted running up them. Her options were few though, so she glanced around from where she stood behind a table leg and prepared to run for it.

"Lunch is almost over, folks!" boomed a voice from behind.

Rein jumped and her vision went white as she bolted back behind the table leg. Had she been spotted?

"Let's prepare to bring in the dishes," the voice continued. "You three, fetch the ingredients for dinner."

Rein's muscles melted, but her trembling continued. She'd gone unnoticed, but this wasn't over yet. Hopefully with three people or more leaving she'd be more likely to dash up the stairs unnoticed as well. She waited for people to exit the kitchen and relished the relief of finally knowing the time of day, thanks to someone shouting it at the top of his lungs. This brought on the realization that she had missed four whole meals. Evidently, she really needed sleep.

When Rein felt that everyone who would leave had left and those who remained behind were significantly occupied, she braced herself and darted up the stairs. She didn't even bother to look over her shoulder to see if she had been spotted. Rather, once she emerged at the top of the staircase, she pounced onto the leg of a console table and then leapt into the leaves of the potted plant beside it. There she waited to confirm that she hadn't been seen before she hopped out and rolled into the tall grass that blanketed the first floor of the White Castle. From there, Rein scurried across the lawn, dashed to Jaska's study, and dove under the closed door.

Rein leaned against the wall inside the study and took a moment to let her heart steady. She had successfully arrived unseen. She could hardly wait to regain her wings; sneaking about would become much easier. Now the question was: What type of book would discuss the information she sought? Perhaps a personal journal or a sacred cult book? It was doubtful that the leader would keep a private journal in his study, so it was probably wiser to start looking for a sacred cult book.

Rein scanned the bottom shelf of Jaska's bookcase, but none of the titles stood out to her. Her eyes slowly climbed higher up the bookcase until finally, on the fourth shelf, she saw a white book titled, *Sweet Suffering Creed*. The word "Creed" stood out to her. Rein scaled up the bookcase to the shelf on which the *Sweet Suffering Creed* rested, taking her time to favor her wounded limbs. Once she had arrived, Rein spat into her hands and rubbed her saliva of stardust all over the book to make it easier to lift. Then she tossed it to the floor and dragged it beneath a side table behind the door.

Rein examined the cover where the silver-leaf title and author were inscribed: "By Jaska Astig." She arched an eyebrow at this discovery and then opened the book to the table of contents. She found her interest increasing exponentially as she read the titles of each chapter: *The Meaning of Life, Your Purpose, How to Be Happy, Family Life, How One Should Live, How One Remains Pure, The Honor of Betrothing, The Honor of Sacrifice, The Solution is War,* and finally, *Bringing Others to the Faith.*

Rein longed to read the entire book simply to satisfy her curiosity, but she couldn't stay in the study if she were to do that. She had to find a place to hide with the book if she wanted to read it. Since the guest rooms seemed to rarely be in use, one of those would probably be a good place to do so. However, the study door was closed and the book was too thick to slip underneath. Rein decided that she would explore the book where she was and as soon as someone entered the study, she would sneak it out the open door, wait until everyone went to bed, and bring it to a guest room. Meanwhile, she needed to find the chapter on Martalitas. Since she remembered that Jaska had mentioned sacrifice, Rein flipped to the chapter on, "The Honor of Sacrifice."

> *Mortalitas Justum is the ceremony during which the Facio Ritus is sacrificed, and must always be the last ceremony of Martalitas.*

Clearly Martalitas was mentioned before this chapter. Rein flipped to the previous chapter: "The Honor of Betrothing."

> *Danzare Ritus is an honorable betrothing ceremony, which takes place at the peak of Martalitas.*

Rein rubbed her face and prayed that Martalitas was explained in the chapter prior. She flipped to the chapter titled, "How One Remains Pure."

> *To live a prosperous and full life, we must remain pure. If we are not pure, Karma will shower his wrath upon us and we will lose our favor with the gods, who bless us continually so long as we are worthy. To maintain our favor, we must participate in Martalitas, which takes place on the first of every other month. Martalitas, a holiday of purification, consists of joyous celebration for the blessings the gods bestow upon us, as well as two honorable ceremonies: Danzare Ritus and Mortalitas Justum.*
>
> *Danzare Ritus is a happy ceremony where the two most favorable children are virtuously betrothed. Through this ceremony, the children are blessed with the promise of favorable and worthy children of their own, and they will have a rich and happy family for the rest of their glorious lives. This ceremony shall be further explained subsequently.*
>
> *Mortalitas Justum is the ceremony of proper purification, where we are to sacrifice the Facio Ritus: the chosen woman of over eighteen years of age to purify the rest of us with her noble death. The Facio Ritus must be a woman due to their unworthy ability to produce life as only the gods are worthy enough of this feat. Thus, the death of the Facio Ritus is to be long and miserable to signify the disappointment we cause*

to the gods with our constant need for purification and our unworthy ability to give life. Mortalitas Justum shall be further explained subsequently.

Rein was horrified and paused to question if she even wanted to read further. When she searched her heart, she found the truth was that no matter how this book made her feel about the despicable nature of this cult's morality, her curiosity would forever torment her if she did not quench it.

Suddenly, the door to the study opened and snapped Rein out of her thoughts. This may be her chance. Rein peered beneath the hinge to find the foyer beyond clear of people, and she was grateful for Jaska leaving the door open. She waited for him to take a seat at his desk and while he shuffled about his deskwork, Rein cautiously brought the book around the door, slowly out of the study, and quietly under the same console table beneath which she had hid only the day before. There, Rein took a moment to breathe. The mere anxiety she suffered every moment in this White Castle could kill her before she ever had the chance to even greet the Mystery Miracle Worker.

Rein decided to leave the book there while she grabbed something to eat from the grand kitchen and wait for the day to end for everyone. As she did so, she pondered on the possibilities of how Martalitas was conducted and plotted how she was going to save Renée. She didn't suppose she'd be able to save her while they transported her to wherever they were going to sacrifice her. This made Rein wonder where they would do this and how? It appeared that she would need to read even further in that cult book whether she desired it or not.

Rein had returned to the console table just in time for Jaska to lead Cloid into his study, and based on his heavy stride he was not in a pleasurable mood. Rein munched on her crumb of banana bread and listened to the ensuing conversation.

"See?" came Jaska's voice. "What happened to it? Did you take it?"

"No, sire. I would've asked for your approval first."

"Well somebody took it, it's clearly no longer in my bookcase!"

"Perhaps Lazar borrowed it?" Cloid suggested.

"Well go find out," Jaska ordered. "We can't have people stealing my books! *Especially* the sacred ones."

"Yes, Your Excellency."

Cloid shuffled by the console table and to Rein's relief, Jaska remained in his study. However, she needed to find a better place to hide the book until that night. Surely once they realized that no one they knew had the book, they'd start looking beneath the furniture. So she scanned the first level of the castle for a better spot. A grin tugged at the corner of her mouth when her eyes fell to the koi pond. This did feel like the most appropriate place to toss the book, but Rein still needed to read it. Perhaps when she was through, she could feed the fish. In the meantime, Rein felt that the least-likely place they would search, at least that night, was behind the firewood.

It was a long distance from the console table to the fireplace by which the wood was stacked. Rein would be open to not only the eyes of the palace staff, but to the small birds which flew about this level of the castle and preyed on insects. It was another stressful situation Rein would have to face, and she knew it wouldn't be the last.

Rein spat all over the book just in case it would offer any more help, snatched a hold of the leather bookmark, and began her trek across the grassy floor, dragging the sacred cult book behind her. She kept a wary eye out for any hungry fowl that would spot her, and eyed the silver and white settee in the drawing room. Here was an ideal place to seek momentary refuge. But the book was heavy and the grass did not provide Rein with a smooth surface. She noticed the very moment the birds caught sight of her, and they watched her closely. They studied her intently. Rein thought her banana bread might shoot back up from her stomach as she waited for one of these feathered predators to make their move, and she didn't even notice her pace slow until she wasn't moving anymore. It was only when she stopped entirely that she endeavored to run toward the settee, though she accomplished more of a "power-walk" rather than a "run."

After maybe three steps, a light-blue sparrow made the first attempt at diving for the wingless pixie. Rein ducked under the sacred book and after feeling the bird collide with the cover, she peered out from beneath and watched for any more attacks. The birds appeared unmoved and uninterested. Rein drew her sword before she emerged and continued her desperate mission to the settee. She accomplished a few more steps before a yellow finch came after her. Rein planted her feet and gripped her sword as she watched the finch draw closer, seemingly slow but swift all at once. Before the finch could snatch her up, Rein drove her blade into the bird's chest. She dropped to her knees beneath it as it soared above and landed in the blades of grass behind her. She panted, surprised at her own success, but there wasn't time to waste. Rein took her sword back, clutched the bookmark with a death grip, and advanced toward the sitting room with deliberation.

When Rein was only steps away from the settee, a pink wren swooped down for her at a speed more alarming than that of the finch or the swallow. In a split-second decision, Rein left the book behind and lunged beneath the seat just as the wren's beak clipped her boot. Rein almost screamed, but caught herself when she realized she was safe. While she still had the chance, she bolted out to snatch the book and hauled it with her beneath the seat just as the wren dove back down for her again. Rein quickly pulled herself together and found no reason to stop here. She lugged the book along to the other end of the settee and dashed under a wingchair with it. Here she opted to wait for the birds to settle before she made her break for the firewood.

Rein found this a prime time to pause further as she spotted Cloid making his way back down the stairwell, and she watched as he approached the study. While it was slightly more difficult to hear him speak with Jaska from this far, Rein still managed to make out the words.

"Sire," came Cloid's voice. "Lazar doesn't have it. He says he doesn't even know what it is."

"This is absurd!" Jaska exclaimed. Shortly he was outside the study yelling at anyone who could hear him. "We must search the palace now! Nobody is to be trusted!"

"Yes, Your Excellency."

As Jaska flailed his arms about, Rein caught sight of something shiny hanging around his neck—the key! She watched as he tucked it back into his white tunic before he returned to his study. Cloid immediately got to work employing a search party for the cult book and Rein knew she had to hide it behind the firewood before the group was assembled. With much struggle, Rein heaved the book behind the large mound of firewood and moments later the first level was busy with palace staff. They didn't seem to be searching the floor, however. Rein assumed they were probably searching each other's rooms investigating who could possibly have taken the book.

While she waited for the situation to calm, Rein thought about how she would get the key from the Grand Master. The easiest way she could think of was if she were to sneak into his bedchamber while he was sleeping and slip it over his head. After all, he probably slept with the thing still attached to his body like a tumor. She would have to find where his bedchamber was located in order to execute such a plan, of course.

Rein decided to take care of that once she finished reading the book. She couldn't have the leader searching for two essential items at the same time. The panic it would cause might hinder her chances at saving Renée. Ironically, Rein figured that the key was in the safest place at the time since Jaska's main concern was the Martalitas celebration. So, when all had gone to bed, she set her plan in motion.

It took perhaps an hour for Rein to lug the sacred book three stories to an empty guest bedroom where she spent most of her days reading it. She quickly adapted to a nocturnal habit, since it seemed as though she was less likely to be caught roaming around the castle while most of the palace staff were sleeping. A couple days later, she found out that she could survive on one burdania petal every other day, and eventually half a petal every other day. It weakened her significantly, but she figured that she could return to her regular petal routine a week before her intended exodus from the lair. That way she had enough strength to escape successfully.

Meanwhile, Rein learned quite a bit about these people, their Sweet Suffering religion, and their culture. It turned out that although they may have strived for purity and honor, they strongly believed in "The Great War," in which they would all take part. "The worthy will establish its supremacy over all the land and the non-believers will convert for a chance at immortality and purity, or their mortal state will take its toll." Fortunately, this war wasn't supposed to happen for another few centuries or so.

Karma was the name of their main god (evidently, they had many). These followers were convinced that they were immortal and only the most impure die, so Rein assumed that Jaska somehow made the elders appear evil and impure somehow. This must be why he wanted access to the Cataras Springs so desperately.

Further into the book, Rein read that around the beginning of time and before women were capable of giving birth, a woman went to a witch on the first day of the month of Alba (the first month of the year), and begged for the ability to give life. The witch, being a woman herself, admired this idea and decided to make a wondrous curse for all women to bear the ability to give life, which she activated two months later. This upset the gods and they made it a law that on the first day of every other month, a woman must be brutally tortured and sacrificed if the people of Xyntriav wished to be pure and live forever in riches and honor. At least, this is what Jaska wished for everyone to believe.

Rein also discovered that Empress Renée was to be sacrificed on a "Ceremonial Stand," which was supposed to be built the day before Martalitas. It was also where the two most favorable children were to be betrothed, all of which was to happen after the, "joyous celebrations." Rein couldn't help but notice that this religion was basically made up of pieces of other religions, customs, and rituals from around the world. She could practically point them out: *this piece is from the old ogre customs in the Farstead Forest, this sounds like a current ritual conducted by the tribes on the Monturian Islands, and this story resembles that of a parable from the religion practiced by Tappurians.*

Jaska Astig had taken these pieces, twisted and tweaked some of them, added a dash of violent envy, sprinkled a few touches of his own creativity, and slapped it with the title, "Sweet Suffering Creed." Rein had to admit that she had underestimated him somewhat; he was a bit more educated than she had originally believed and she could only imagine there were similarities in this cult to other beliefs around the world of which she was unaware. She wasn't too pleased with this, however. Fools may be worrisome because they're careless, but the intelligent are frightening because they know what they're doing.

After half a month, Rein decided to take a break from reading this disturbing and depressing book and searched for Jaska's bedchambers. She had paid attention to the events of each day for the past four weeks, so she was aware of Jaska's daily schedule. She was also relieved to learn that he still wore the key like a powerful pendant around his neck as Empress Renée had. This man may be smart with his vast studies, but he was certainly not wise with some of his important decisions. One night, when he made his way to his chambers, Rein kept her distance while she followed Jaska and discovered that he slept behind a pair of large platinum doors. Now she knew where to go to take the key back when she was finally ready to do so.

Rein finished the book a week before Martalitas and proudly tossed it into the koi pond while Jaska prepared for bed. The wounds on her leg and arm were nearly healed at this point and she could move about with a little more ease, though she still suffered from some fatigue due to cutting back on the burdania petals. She took her time as she made her way to Jaska's chambers once the entire castle had settled down for the night, and hid inside a potted plant where she waited for him to fall asleep. As Rein had predicted, he kept the key around his neck while he slept. He also left the dim light of a lantern on to silently lull him to sleep.

While Rein waited impatiently for Jaska's soft snores, she glimpsed around the chamber to keep herself entertained. The bedchamber appeared similar to the rest of the palace, with grass covering the white floors, plants hanging from the ceiling, and flowers filling the room with their aromas. Rein also noticed a large, silver-framed portrait of Jaska hung above his bed with pride and she rolled her eyes in disgust.

Finally, Rein heard Jaska begin to lightly snore. Now was the time to steal the key back and make a run for it. She darted to the massive bed and shimmied up the silver bedpost. There, she waited for a moment to verify that the Grand Master was asleep for certain. When she observed the subtle rise and fall of his chest, Rein cautiously crept over the folds of the white silk sheets, slowly making her way up to Jaska where she searched around for the knot in the broken chain of the necklace. However, she found that Jaska had replaced the chain with a thick, leather string and she couldn't find the knot or clip. Her arms trembled with fiery adrenaline knowing that Jaska could wake up at any moment. Rather than risk moving the string to find where the ends connected, Rein brought out her knife. While she stepped on the string with one foot and used her hand to keep it steady, she began to saw at it. The sound of the blade rubbing against the leather seemed louder than she thought was possible, which sparked the urge to hack faster. Then the string broke with a startling SNAP and to Rein's horror, Jaska stirred.

Chapter Eleven

Rein didn't breathe for a moment. The chamber grew hot as she watched Jaska intently. His head turned toward her and Rein prepared to run, but then he stopped moving. Rein's taut muscles ached as she stood motionless like one of Jaska's marble statues. When the Grand Master snored again, Rein rubbed the sweat from her forehead and tried not to exhale too loud. *Keep it together,* she thought.

Then suddenly Jaska rolled over and Rein dove beneath a silver pillow. The cool satin felt relieving as she waited for confirmation that it was safe to emerge, but her heartbeat pounded painfully when she realized that Jaska had rolled over onto the key. She squirmed and wriggled around beneath the pile of silver, white, and gray pillows to make her way behind Jaska, and the weight on top of her increased her level of fatigue. Before she could emerge from the mound of cushions, she had to take a moment to rest. Rein needed to save her energy to make her escape from the chambers with the heavy key, so this wasn't any time to be impatient and over-strain herself. Then, she realized that she could tug on his hair from where she lay. The first tug only got him to twitch. The second tug got him to successfully roll back over to reveal the key. Now Rein had to inch her way back to her original spot.

Rein waited to hear Jaska snore again while she rested and checked on the status of the key. It was nearly free of the string and all she had to do was grab it and go. Perhaps there was no need to wait around for more strength and she had enough energy to make it out after all. Rein pushed herself back to her feet and crept over to the key. Then she made a run for it. She snatched the key up and jumped off the bed. However, the knot got caught in the loop of the key and she ended up taking the string with her. Without glancing back to see if the movement from the string awoke the Grand Master, Rein dove under the door and exited the bedchamber for good.

Rein kept the key beside her alcove behind the counter in the grand kitchen. She would've liked to bring it inside with her, but the tiny hole in the wall wouldn't fit both of them. She could hear the echoes of Jaska's rage the next day when he realized the key had disappeared. She watched from beneath the settee as Jaska marveled at the sight of his holy book being fished out of the koi pond. She could tell he suspected that this and the loss of the key were connected. Rein wasn't sure, but she wondered if Jaska suspected that she was the one doing all the stealing and dumping. It didn't matter now that she had the key and she knew that Jaska would never be able to catch her, but she was curious about his thoughts.

At this point, Rein had returned to eating a burdania petal a day and she could feel a major difference in herself. It made her longing for wings increase aggressively. After three centuries without them she had already cried her fair share of tears, but being this close to success she felt that more tears were unnecessary. She had a plan and she was executing it one step at a time.

Martalitas Eve eventually came and Rein perched herself on a gargoyle butterfly which overlooked the flowery courtyard. Here she watched the citizens of the underground lair set up for the celebration. She used Jaska's leather string to secure the key to her back as she witnessed everything she had read about unfold. Unfortunately, she still didn't know how Jaska planned to sacrifice the empress. The way his holy book said to do it wouldn't work on Renée since she was a naiad and water is hard to cut, burn, rip apart, and stab. So Rein was prepared to think and act quickly when the appropriate time arose.

Rein watched as the citizens built the ceremonial stand on an open patch of grass while others tended to the surrounding, brightly colored flowers. On a separate patch of grass, they placed five exceedingly long tables and prepared them for a sizeable feast. On the lower level of the ceremonial stand, they set a separate table, which Rein assumed was reserved for Jaska Astig.

Finally, the day of Martalitas had arrived and an abundance of food was laid out on the tables for the feast.

Rein watched some of the citizens roast a hippopotamus over a large fire while others carved happy faces into watermelons and cantaloupe with their children. Once the hippopotamus was done, they set one of the watermelons in its mouth and placed it on the center table. There were salads, pies, cakes, mashed potatoes, casseroles, different flavors of gravy and glaze, shish kebabs, roasted beasts, grilled fish, stewed vegetables, fresh fruits—Rein had never seen such a fine-looking feast!

It wasn't long before the residents of the underground lair sat at these tables dressed in white and filled their plates with food. The Grand Master sat alone at the single table on the ceremonial stand dressed in a massive white and silver robe with runes embroidered on the large sleeves. He had his servants bring his plates and drinks to him and once everyone had food in front of them, Jaska stood and pounded a pearl staff on the stand to get everyone's attention.

"Ladies and gentlemen, my dear children," he said. "Today is not just any Martalitas, but the last one of the year, which makes it the most significant. Today, we purify ourselves in preparation for the next coming year. And in honor of this special, fifth Martalitas, the gods have sent us a most precious sacrifice to ensure our complete purification. This is evidence that we have been greatly blessed. Together, we have made the gods smile upon us—a true reason for celebration. Therefore, let us celebrate! Happy Martalitas!"

Everyone cheered and immediately proceeded to devour their food.

The feast took much time to finish. All Rein could do was merely watch these people eat with her elbow on her knee and her head in her hand, but then she caught sight of something that slightly disturbed her. Many of these practitioners brought their pets out with them and some of these pets appeared to be tiny, plushy bears with large, black eyes. They walked on all fours and wagged their stubby little tails. What were these creatures? Rein had never seen them before and she winced at the sight of them.

Moments later, one of the most frightful things Rein had ever witnessed appeared before her eyes. A party of beings exited the palace with exaggerated face paint, big, bright hair made into strange hairstyles, and frilly outfits so brightly colored they burned her eyes. Rein nearly screamed when they turned and showed their exotic, taboo faces, and she watched as they performed an eerie dance for everyone's entertainment. Each step was emphasized and they clawed the air as if they fought to escape some confined space. Rein kept a hand over her mouth and watched the episode unfold before her eyes as if she were watching a fiery hailstorm.

After that horrifying spectacle was over, Rein nearly lost the nerve to go and save the empress. What if these things were still present at the time of the sacrifice? Rein prayed they wouldn't be around, but it didn't seem like matters would play out that way. The beings remained for the joyous celebration, which began next. The people got up from their tables and approached the center of Jaska's courtyard. Loud and overly-cheerful music began to play and the people started to dance. Rein did her best not to watch the colorful beings and their unusual jig. It seemed as though at this point, Mortalitas Justum would never take place.

Rein decided to turn her back to the scene and wait for the music to stop, half out of boredom and half out of disgust. In this moment, an alarming pang shot from her left hand all the way up to her shoulder. She clutched her arm and held it against her body, waiting for the pain to go away. The burn slowly receded to an ache and she removed her black glove to examine the mark of her oath to Captain Tzatara. The faint gold glow gleamed brighter and she swallowed her panic. The captain must be on his way to the Springs. She hadn't much time. If Rein failed to rescue the empress today, she may just have to take the key and leave her behind. She heaved a heavy sigh as she felt her burden grow denser.

At long last, it was time for Danzare Ritus. Rein finally paid attention as she was interested in watching this ritual she had read about. Jaska stood on the lower level of the ceremonial stand with his staff in hand, and the citizens of the underground lair gathered around.

"Come closer, everyone," Jaska said. "Up close and personal. It is time to announce the honorable children for the Danzare Ritus! I have their names right here. Come closer. They are... Bobby and Kelly!"

The announcement was followed by praise and two couples rushed away to prepare their children for the ceremony. Rein assumed that since everyone lived in the same city and there was no last name for these children,

Jaska must somehow make sure no two people had the same name. There was no other way that Rein could imagine telling people apart here.

Now Rein had to wait for these children to get ready for their ceremony. Her patience was wearing thin. To help herself, she tried imagining different ways Jaska could come up with to kill a naiad, but nothing came to mind. She rubbed her face in annoyance and waited for the children to return.

Unaware to Rein, the mysterious man in the silver cloak was present at this time, however he waited in the dark allies of the city to remain hidden from the commotion in the courtyard. He gazed around as if searching for something until he spotted the tiny speck of light on the butterfly gargoyle. As he lifted his head, some light finally entered the hood of his cloak to reveal his wicked grin. Satisfied, he patiently awaited the end of the holiday.

Eventually, Bobby returned dressed in white and baby blue. He was led up to the ceremonial stand and stood beneath Jaska to wait for his future bride. She appeared a while after, also dressed in white and with the added touch of daisies. She was led to the beginning of the grassy patch and awaited her cue to approach Jaska and Bobby. A torturous wind instrument screeched a tone that cut the air and Kelly slowly walked toward the ceremonial stand. Rein covered her ears and winced at the racket. The blaring noise ceased only after Kelly stood beside Bobby. Rein could finally pay attention as the children joined hands and Jaska began to speak.

"My people! We are gathered together on this day of Martalitas to celebrate the event of Danzare Ritus, where we join together two noble children and betroth them. When they become of age, they are to return here and marry. Bobby, by the power bestowed upon me by the gods themselves, I hereby confer onto you the honor of marrying Kelly once you reach the age of sixteen. If you attempt to defy this order from the gods, you will be sacrificed on the following Martalitas as a dishonorable, male victim. Do you understand these terms?"

"I do," Bobby replied.

"Kelly, by the power bestowed upon me by the gods themselves, I hereby confer onto you the honor of marrying Bobby once you reach the age of sixteen. If you attempt to defy this order from the gods, you will be sacrificed on the following Martalitas as a dishonorable victim. Do you understand these terms?"

"I do," said Kelly.

"I now declare these children to be officially betrothed!" Jaska announced and the city erupted in applause and cheers. "Bobby, Kelly, understand that because you two have been chosen to be betrothed on this Martalitas Day, your lives are blessed to be rich and pure. May your children be as noble as you are and may the rest of your lives be as joyous as the holidays."

The crowd once more gave a round of applause.

Now if Rein had read correctly, the sacrifice was next. The ceremonial stand and the area around it were cleared and cleaned for the next event and everyone went away to prepare. Rein inched herself near the edge of the white stone butterfly wing and watched intently as Cloid and Lazar prepared a pile of kindling on the upper level of the ceremonial stand, after which they brought out a cauldron with a large, heavy lid. For a moment, Rein was confused. Hadn't the feast ended? The sacrifice should be next. Then it dawned on her: they were going to boil the empress! How was Rein going to stop it? The cauldron appeared obnoxiously heavy. The only way she could think of saving the empress was if she tipped the cauldron over after they poured her into it… unless she found a way to collapse the stand. No other option presented itself and Rein didn't have much time to carefully devise any other strategy. She would have to give it a try.

Chapter Twelve

Rein scaled down the castle walls. The mysterious man watched as the tiny speck of light weaved about bushes and tall flowers, sneaking up to the ceremonial stand as quickly as she could without wings. Once Rein reached it, the mysterious man lost sight of her and had to find a new hiding spot. Fortunately, the city's residents were currently located in the Grand Master's courtyard, so sneaking about wasn't too difficult for him, though he did decide on a much closer refuge. He tucked himself away behind a tree and a few bushes where he could watch Rein execute her mission.

Meanwhile, Rein shimmied up one of the legs of the stand and used her sword to saw away at it. She didn't want to saw all the way through, of course; just enough to make the stand fairly precarious for when they brought out the empress. As Rein did this, Cloid and Lazar hung the cauldron in place and started the fire. By the time the blaze was satisfactory, Rein had made a slit in only one leg of the stand. However, it wasn't enough for Rein. She shimmied up the second leg on the same side of the stand and cut away at that one as well. All the exertion and anxiety sent her body temperature soaring. She paused and threw off her coat, then continued to saw madly at the wooden leg.

Still unconvinced in the surety of her plan, Rein untied the key from her back, hid it beneath her coat, and climbed up the stand to saw at the device which held the cauldron over the fire. Even though the flames nearly licked her body, Rein was thankful for the fire; it hid her light and made it more difficult for her to be seen. Rein finished executing her plan only moments before Jaska took his place on stage and announced the next event to all his people.

"Ladies and gentlemen, my children! The time has come for Mortalitas Justum!"

The crowd cheered as Rein rapidly made her way down the stand. In her hurry, her arm snagged violently on a splinter which caused her to lose her grip and she tumbled the rest of the way down into the grass.

"This is the most vital part of this magnificent holiday, and for the fifth Martalitas, the most vital part of the year. To acknowledge this, our sacrifice is someone quite special."

Rein found herself face to face with one of those eerie, tiny bears, which appeared much more unsettling up close. The two of them stared at each other for what felt like an eternity before the bear sniffed her. Rein pushed herself against the leg of the stand in a desperate attempt to back away from the animal.

"Nice... creature," Rein said. Perhaps flattery would keep it from eating her. "I—I'm a friend. If you don't be nice to me, I'll have to kill you, you know. You don't want that right?"

"Ladies and gentlemen," Jaska continued. "I give you our Facio Ritus: a naiad!"

The crowd cheered and Rein glanced over her shoulder to observe Cloid and Lazar carrying a large vase onto the ceremonial stand. The wood cracked, squeaked, and creaked; a good sign so far, but the tiny bear kept sniffing and pawing at Rein.

"Go away," Rein said. "It's going to fall, we don't want to be here when that happens."

That was when the tiny creature bared its many sharp teeth at Rein with a sinister smile. Rein was seconds from screaming, but right as the servants poured the empress into the cauldron, the wooden holder snapped. It crumbled into the ceremonial stand with a thundering BANG and CRASH, and the stand itself snapped and cracked where Rein had cut into it.

While the tiny bear was distracted by the clamorous commotion above, Rein jumped out of the way with the presence of mind to grab her coat and the key. Just as the stand collapsed into a pile of splinters onto the creature, she dove into a flower bed that was barely out of the way of the debris. Rein didn't waste time staring that the mess or the panicked residents of the realm. She quickly replaced her coat and kept an eye out for the empress. Rein felt lucky to catch sight of the empress as she poured out of the cauldron and into the creek in the center of the realm. The wingless pixie frantically fastened the key to her back and ran off with the hope to somehow keep up with Empress Renée.

The journey to the other end of the city was a long one, but Rein was so anxious to get out of there, she would have sprinted ten times the distance if she had to. The horrible weight of the key on her back kept her speed slow and used up twice the amount of energy it usually took her to run. She ignored the ache in her legs and the burn in her lungs. She would not pause to rest until she had finally exited the underground lair.

Suddenly, Rein felt herself being scooped up from the ground by a hand which secured her arms to her sides and she released a despondent scream. She had lost! After everything she had put up with that entire month, she had failed! To Rein's shock however, the bearer of the hand was gentle and ran toward the exit of the realm. Rein tried to catch a glimpse of his face, but the hood of his silver cloak hid it in an unyielding shadow. Though he seemed to also want out of the underground lair, his mysterious intentions kept her on edge. Would he let her free after they exited, or would he take her somewhere else? Or would he steal her key? There was no telling what would happen and Rein prepared for the worst.

The mysterious man flew up the steps and sprinted out of the cave, never once uttering a word to Rein or showing his face. Once they were out in the surrounding woods on the surface of Arcor Island, he set Rein down on a tree branch a few feet outside the cave and made his way toward Main Port. Rein watched him, wide-eyed.

She made sure she still had the key with her and that he hadn't taken it without her noticing. It was bizarre that he had hardly made an attempt. Perhaps he was ignorant to what the key unlocked. Rein pushed the oddity out of her mind and searched around for any sign of the empress. She spotted movement in the mud and grass that coursed from inside the cave to the direction of the shore.

"Renée!" she called.

Empress Renée stopped and rose up to her waist to address her pixie friend.

"I can't do this, Rein!" she cried. "I'm done, this is too much! I have to return home!"

"I understand, Renée, it was rough in there," the pixie replied. "But don't go home yet!"

"I can't stay on this island for another minute!"

"Nor can I, let's meet on Contrariet," Rein offered. "Can you meet me on Contrariet?"

"What's that?"

"It's the next island on the chain, northwest. Will you please meet me there? Just humor me. I did just save your life, after all."

The empress sobbed in reply. "If you insist!"

Rein lassoed a bird and used it to fly to the next island on the Continent Island chain. All the way there she prayed that the empress wouldn't change her mind. She knew that they would fight over the key, but Rein hoped that if she was able to spend some time with the empress, she could convince her that the Cataras Springs weren't what she needed to find happiness. Contrariet may not be the most optimal place to attempt such a feat, but it was arguably better than Arcor.

Once she landed on Contrariet, Rein set the bird free and waited anxiously by the shore for the empress to appear. The Northern sun was already setting, which compelled Rein to wonder how much time Renée had left. She removed the key from her back and examined it: the rose bud had almost finished blooming. Time was scarce or them both.

Finally, Empress Renée appeared on the shore and looked back over her shoulder in the direction of Arcor. Then she collapsed on the beach and held her face in her hands. Rein hurried down the tree and crawled over the white sand to approach her.

"Renée!" she called.

"Oh Rein!" the empress sobbed. "Thank you so much! *Spells*, it feels wonderful to be out of that underworld!"

"I couldn't agree more," said Rein. "Listen, it's getting dark. Why don't we find some shelter where we can relax safely?"

"I don't know, Rein," the empress replied. "I didn't expect this scavenger hunt to be so torturous. Even if I find the Springs, they can't make me happy now."

This way of thinking couldn't be good for Nadia either. Rein felt like she trod on thin ice at this point. "I can't argue with that, but perhaps we can discuss other ways you can be happy?"

"After what happened on Arcor, I could never be happy. It's hopeless! I was trapped in a box of torture devices for months, Rein!"

"It's only been one month, Renée." Rein tried to be soft and empathetic. "But I understand, it was a horrible experience. You'll need time to recover. But look at you, Renée, you're flustered. You're a mess. You don't want to return to the Obsidian Palace like this."

The empress glared at the pixie, but she said nothing in reply. She was supposed to be the mother of the heir to the five oceans, and she was supposed to care about saving this heir. Nadia's real mother would follow Rein and discuss other ways to save her. Perhaps she could humor Rein for a bit while doing exactly what the pixie suggested: recover.

"Follow me," Rein coaxed. "I recall a cave where we can spend the night."

"You've been here before?" the empress asked.

"Centuries ago," Rein answered. "But I doubt the cave is gone."

After some consideration, the empress nodded and held out her hand to Rein. Once the pixie climbed onto Renée's palm, the empress wearily pushed herself to her feet and allowed her friend to direct her around the thick forest where the leaves on the trees were different shades of bright pink and orange. It was a lively forest full of cheerful tweets and chitters that seemed to calm Renée a bit. She felt her anxiety melt away and looked forward to spending a night here. Then she glanced at her pixie friend whose face was crinkled with worry.

"What's wrong?" Renée asked.

The pixie glanced at her with concerned surprise. "Are you not paying attention?"

The empress scanned her surroundings and that's when she observed the piles of dead, half-eaten, half-decomposed animals which spotted the forest ground. Then she noticed how their odor fumed the air and the farther they progressed into the forest, the stronger the stench became.

"Only the strongest survive nights on Contrariet," Rein explained. "After the suns set, all the creatures go mad and attack one another. That's why we need to get to this cave quickly."

As twilight gave way to night, the empress noticed that all the plant-life began to glow in neon colors. Rein recognized this was the sign that they hadn't much time to find safety, but she knew where they were on the island and it wasn't long before they finally arrived at the mossy cave she had mentioned.

"Here," Rein pointed. "There's a large rock inside you can roll in front of the opening and we'll be safe from the animals when they go mad."

The empress set the pixie on a rock outside the cave. "Very well. I'll meet you inside."

Rein watched as the empress approached a fruit tree and reached to pick some fruit. "The food on this island isn't safe to eat," she warned.

"Then what do all these animals eat?" the empress asked.

"Well the food, and then each other. It's the food that makes them go mad."

"Really," the empress challenged. "And how are you so sure?"

"I told you I've visited the island before," Rein replied. "I've eaten the fruit, and the night I spent here was wild. The next night I didn't eat the food and I had to take refuge from those which had."

"Well what do you expect me to eat then?" the empress asked.

"You didn't eat anything on your way here?"

"No, I was focused on arriving."

"You still could've found something to eat on the way. You hadn't eaten for a whole month, I would think that food would be your priority once you were free."

"What do you know about one's priorities after gaining freedom?" the empress snapped. "Have you ever been locked in a box for a month?"

"No, just as you've never had your wings slowly torn from your body!" Rein snapped back. "We've both experienced our fair share of suffering, *Your Majesty*! So don't try telling me I'm ignorant to how you feel!"

The empress glared at Rein, removed a gleaming pink fruit from the glowing tree above her, and deliberately took a spiteful bite out of it. Rein's eyes widened and she sucked in a panicked breath. How long had it taken for the fruit to affect her all those years ago? She would have to seek refuge from the empress in a few hours. Hopefully she could strike an effective conversation with her in the meantime.

"Very well, Empress," Rein said. "Let's close you inside the cave while we wait for it to take effect."

"Oh relax, Little Pixie," said the empress as she entered the cave. "I can maintain my faculties."

Inside, they discovered a few humanoid skeletons surrounded by an obnoxious stench.

"Friends of yours?" asked the empress as she struggled to roll the boulder in front of the opening.

Rein took a seat on a rock beside the entrance to the cave to maintain her distance from the naiad. "No, these are more recent than three centuries." She had packed a few bites of food for herself from the underground lair and decided to eat it along with her burdania petals.

The empress sat against the wall and finished her fruit. "Hm, I wonder what got to them."

"Each other, most likely," Rein replied. Considering that the empress appeared to be her normal self, Rein opted to pretend that all was well and they still planned to visit the Mystery Miracle Worker. "So listen, if we make it off the island tomorrow, we should wait on Incaendium before we continue to Roznova."

"Why?" the empress asked.

Rein couldn't gage how the empress felt based on this question alone, but the fact that she didn't shut the idea down immediately was promising. "Because every ten minutes, Roznova is surrounded by a large explosion of fire. It's so hot that the water around the island is in a chronic boil. So we should wait on Incaendium for the fire to erupt and then head over to Roznova immediately. By the time we reach Roznova, the fire will have stopped. Then we have ten minutes to find the Mystery Miracle Worker's lair."

"Wonderful," replied the empress. She took another bite of her glowing fruit.

Rein had only managed to obtain two words from the empress, but neither of them were "no," and she felt it safe to assume that they were still visiting the Mystery Miracle Worker on the morrow. Now to broach another subject. "So how did you end up marrying the emperor of the five oceans?"

Renée glanced at the pixie, suspicious. "A long time ago, my family had believed I was good for nothing. All my brothers and sisters had been successful in their marriages, and due their success they obtained the love and attention of my parents. One day I managed an invitation to a gala at the palace and that's where I met the emperor. I struck up a conversation and the rest is history. It was nice to get away from the family finally."

"He seems like a decent fellow for marrying you even though you're barren," said Rein.

The empress gave her a fleeting glance. "He didn't know."

Rein swallowed her disproval. "What?"

The empress sighed. "I'll explain if you swear an oath of silence."

Rein gaped at the empress and nodded. "Yes, of course."

"It's estimated that almost half of the ocean's population is infertile," the empress explained. "When naiads reach twenty years of age, we take fertility tests. Of course, I was required to prove my fertility after Jaskaran and I became engaged. So I paid a friend of mine for her fertility test and I promised my family riches for their silence. I showed the test to the imperial court and Jaskaran and I were married.

Afterward, I feigned an injury and blamed my infertility on that. It's no issue though; with that ceremony we were able to obtain an heir."

Rein tried desperately to hide her judgment. "How does that ceremony work?"

The empress glanced at Rein and then cast her eyes down at the floor of the cave. Outside, the bloodthirsty roars of the predators and the whimpering cries of the prey filled the tense silence, but the empress didn't seem to notice any of it. Her head felt fuzzy, and remembering the fact that Nadia was not her child made her stomach wretch. She opted to take advantage of Rein's ignorance on ocean customs.

"We..." the empress began. How could she make it seem like Nadia was as close to being her daughter as she could without having actually birthed her? "We chose Nadia from an orphanage. Then with the help of the miracle worker, my blood and Jaskaran's blood flows through Nadia's veins. It's a long, meticulous, complicated ceremony."

"Really?" Rein asked, iffy. "I thought you adopted Nadia from a nephew, making her already royal by blood. The ceremony was simply to make her heir."

"Where did you hear that?" asked the empress.

"From Queen Tiana."

"She must be mistaken. Jaskaran is an only child, he has no brothers and therefore no nephews."

"Oh..." Rein narrowed her eyes at the empress, but opted to let it go and moved on. "So when did you become unhappy?"

"I was always unhappy, Rein."

"Why didn't your marriage to Jaskaran change that? Clearly, you put a lot of effort into becoming empress and you accomplished it. Your success didn't make you happy?"

"It did for some time," the empress confessed. She tossed the core of her fruit at the skull of one of the skeletons. "I don't know when it all hit dark depths again. It just did."

"You never thought about it? You never tried to learn what sparked it?"

The empress shrugged. "There was nothing to think about. I suppose it's simply the fact that I've always been second or less in everyone's eyes. I'm an afterthought; a backup plan in case the first few ideas aren't as entertaining."

Rein chewed the last of her burdania petal in thought. "Have you tried being more active as empress?"

"How do you mean?"

"Support your husband in his role. I'm sure there are some political matters you can handle yourself. Maybe once you've succeeded in some meaningful changes in the empire you'll have a grand sense of accomplishment *and* others will notice your achievements this time. After that, you won't be second fiddle anymore."

"Second what?"

"Second place, you'll get more recognition."

The empress simply sat there glaring at the ground with an irritated expression on her face. She could feel herself fuming, and she couldn't explain why. Perhaps it was this pixie's words that were getting on her nerves. "Perhaps if the Cataras Springs don't work, I'll see what I can do."

Rein sat in thought for a moment. "So, you think that if you drink from the Spring of Healing, you can provide Jaskaran with a real heir and be happy?"

The empress's heart skipped a beat. "Nadia is a real heir."

"You know what I mean, Renée."

The empress hesitated. "I want to save Nadia. But perhaps I can drink from the spring as well, that would be beneficial."

"But it sounds like there's something else that's making you upset," said Rein. "Something more that the Cataras Springs won't help."

"There is nothing else, Rein," the empress snapped.

Rein studied her for a moment. She thought about keeping her next words to herself, but she couldn't help asking. "Is it Nadia who makes you feel second?"

"Enough, Rein!" the empress hollered. "I will save Nadia! I will show the empire that I do love her, that her poor health is not on me, and they will see that it is because of me that she survives!"

"All right, all right," said Rein. "I wish you all the luck in the world then, Renée."

The empress pouted in reply. How dare this pixie challenge her intentions. Of all the nerve. She sat there, arms crossed over her chest, with a fleeting glare at Rein every once in a while.

Rein ignored her and sharpened her knife with a rock. She wanted to continue their conversation about finding joy for Nadia's sake, but something stopped her. The empress's mood? No, Rein would normally continue pressing the empress regardless, it was something else. Perhaps the Cataras Springs might be what this sad naiad needed. Maybe the Spring of Healing could heal the empress's mind. Was sorrow something that could be healed?

Meanwhile, the empress listened to the scraping of the rock against Rein's tiny blade. It had a rhythm, a beat. It was constant and got louder, scratching like a fork on a porcelain dish. The racket made her teeth cringe.

"Cut it out!" the empress shouted.

Rein glared at her and put the rock down. She resorted to playing with her knife in silence while the empress continued to seethe. The empress heaved a restless sigh. Rein glanced at her to see if she had anything to say, but the air remained still. The empress sighed again, which began to annoy Rein, but the pixie just nibbled on a breadcrumb and held her tongue. The empress gave a final, heavy sigh and then shot to her feet.

"I am so sick of just sitting in here!" she shrieked. Then she approached the boulder blocking the entrance.

"Renée, no!" Rein cried. "It's just the food, remember?"

The empress leaked between the wall and the boulder and then took form again beyond the cave where all the raging animals stopped in mid-devour to look at her with bloody entrails dripping from their jaws. The wolves, foxes, and even squirrels immediately became more interested in the empress and slowly left their previous prey to zero in on her. The empress couldn't explain it, but she felt no fear; only an insuppressible wrath that these beasts would even consider the thought of hunting her. What gave them the right, and on whose orders?

Inside the cave, Rein pulled her coat tighter around her glowing body and debated going out to do what she could to protect the empress. She gnashed her teeth against the realization that she would regret it if she made no effort, and squeezed herself between the wall and the boulder. Outside she watched as a variety of predatory creatures slowly prowled up to the empress, who seemed rather enraged that this could be happening. Rein couldn't understand why the empress was so shocked after her numerous warnings that this was what took place at night on Contrariet. Though she had to admit, Rein recalled little of how she felt the night she ate the fruit of the island.

"Stand back!" Renée demanded, but the animals continued to approach her.

"Renée, just head to Roznova!" Rein whispered.

"I said stay away! *Why aren't you listening to me*?"

The empress attacked the animals, kicking and punching them all with a continuous war cry. The animals tried to bite and claw her, but their teeth went straight through her like water. Rein knew the beasts would figure this out soon enough and try to drink her. So the pixie jumped on one predator at a time, clutching their fur, stabbing them in the back of their necks and behind their ears with her knife. The empress was a fine distraction. When all the animals which survived had fled, Rein and Renée looked at each other.

"What did you do that for?" the empress spat. "I wanted to take care of them all myself!"

Rein simply walked back into the cave.

"Stop ignoring me!" the empress shouted. Then with the power of the pent-up rage inside her, she rolled the large rock aside to reveal the cave. "*Talk to me!*"

"Not until we're off this island," Rein replied calmly. "Would you mind replacing that before you lure more predators toward us?"

"No, we're leaving *immediately*," said the empress. "I can't stand another second on this island, and I'm taking this with me."

Empress Renée snatched Rein and untied the key from the pixie's back.

"Unhand me!" Rein cried. "You have some nerve! Let me go!"

"You have no need for this," said the empress. "I'll see you soon."

"How do you expect me head over there when all the birds are off their rocker?"

"Very well, you can meet me there tomorrow then," said the empress.

"You're just going to leave me here?" Though Rein understood that the empress was inhibited by the fruit of the island, she struggled to wrap her head around the fact that she might be left behind.

"You survived the island before," the empress argued. "You can do so again."

"I had wings then!"

"You've lived without for three centuries."

"In Maja!"

"Enough with the drama, Rein. You'll figure something out, I'm sure."

With that, the empress melted into the ground and left Rein behind with the raging, raving beasts.

Chapter Thirteen

Rein climbed above the cave where she and the empress had previously taken refuge and frantically scanned the island, trying desperately to remember where else she had stayed centuries ago, but her mind came up blank. Though, she realized that she could use a better, higher view of the island, and perhaps that could jog her memory. So she quickly climbed back down and dodged a few rabid creatures as she bolted to a tree and shot up its trunk. She nearly collided with a woodpecker when she got to a satisfying height, which immediately attacked her with its beak. After narrowly avoiding its savage strikes, Rein slashed its throat and continued to the cusp of a branch. Now that she had a better view, she scanned the island again and spotted a large black void approximately thirty yards away where nothing around glowed, shined, or gleamed. From what Rein could tell, it appeared to be void of wildlife as well. She didn't recall this spot from her last trip to Contrariet, but something about it screamed, "sanctuary!"

Rein stumbled into a squirrel on the way back down the tree and they fell to the ground together. They wrestled among the leaves and blood-soaked soil, clawing frantically at each other in a mad effort for victory. The squirrel tore at Rein's outfit and Rein ripped off clumps of its fur until she was finally able to kill it with her knife. There was no time to rest. She sprinted in the direction of the void and tried to remain hidden by the glowing light of the shrubs and bushes, but there came a point where she had no choice but to run back out into the open.

While she passed through, Rein was attacked by a ravenous moth, which she discovered to be more difficult to kill than a squirrel or bird as it fluttered back and forth. When she finally managed to slice it in half with her sword, she heard the horrific hum of a cluster of butterflies hovering above her. A new form of dread overcame Rein that almost confirmed her doom. She scrambled away in a mad frenzy and dove among some rocks and a log while the butterfly colony fought to reach her. Rein stabbed at them through a crevasse, but there was little room to move. The most she could do was wait for the butterflies to grow weary and fly away. At the same time, there was always the possibility that they might wait for her to emerge so they could overtake her then.

Eventually, the colony did flutter away in search of easier prey, and Rein was barely able to stick her head between the rocks and log to see where they flew. Once she surmised that they had given up on her completely, she established which direction she had been running, squeezed out of her hiding spot, and raced toward the void again, her heartbeat in sync with her pace.

At last Rein made it to her destination, but she was hesitant to enter. She hid in a bright pink shrub and surveyed the area for a moment, panting madly. She found it to be a large mushroom field, completely empty of any sign of life, which was suspicious. With her knife and sword at hand, she cautiously entered the field and prepared herself for an attack. She made it all the way to the center of this dark circle without any interference—a good sign so far.

Rein chose the largest mushroom in the field and, while remaining vigilant, carved out a small alcove in it with her knife. Then, she found some poison ivy and carefully placed it all around the mushroom to protect herself from any curious creatures. After that, she tended to the wounds she had received from her battles, finished sharpening her knife, vowed to never forgive Empress Renée for this, and then eventually fell asleep.

Empress Renée spent the remainder of that night beneath Contrariet fighting her uncontrollable animosity like a freed lunatic. The fury failed to cease until the light of the Southern sun slowly stretched over the horizon. The sensation of wrath gradually melting from her mind like ice melts into streams was an odd one that she would've liked to experience again someday. It felt relieving, healing, renewing, and it continued to recede for what seemed like almost an hour. It wasn't until she had completely regained her faculties that Renée noticed an immense flare miles away. As she approached it, she learned this flare was created by the ring of fire which surrounded the island of Roznova. She felt her heart leap into her throat upon this realization.

Renée anxiously flowed through the boiling water as quickly as she could so as not to evaporate, and then shored. Thick steam rose from her body as she rushed farther inland in a desperate search of the Mystery Miracle Worker's lair. The island was covered in steam and smoke, and the smell of forest fire filled the air. But even with this strange climate, the land was blanketed with vibrant vegetation, which made it difficult for Renée to see a reasonable distance ahead of her. The heat which conquered the air was dangerous and she was aware that she couldn't spend too much time out in the open, but her panic made it challenging for her to remember the description of the lair she had been provided.

Soon, Renée heard voices ahead and spotted a young woman, perhaps in her late twenties, dressed in dark yet colorful clothing that jingled when she moved. Half of her face was hidden by her long-brimmed hat and she carried a basket of herbs and vegetables on her arm. The empress's eyes widened when she spotted a king cobra slithering up to the woman. Renée almost shouted to alarm her, but the woman spoke first.

"Come along, Stephocra. You ate yesterday and I'm finished."

Renée watched as the woman reached her free arm out toward the cobra so that it may wrap around her bicep. Then she stood up straight and glanced in the direction of the empress.

"You too, Empress Renée," the woman called. "I am the Mystery Miracle Worker you search for. Make haste before the flames erupt again."

Renée was shocked, but she obeyed and followed the Mystery Miracle Worker to a small hill. The woman brushed aside some wet moss to reveal the opening to a cave and gestured for Renée to enter. Once inside, she pushed a large boulder in front of the entrance just as the island was surrounded in fire which extended fifty feet above the forest. Then the Miracle Worker took a torch in her hand and led Renée deeper into the cave. No one spoke until they passed through a doorway to enter a small lair where the woman let Stephocra slither onto a leafless black tree in a corner of the cozy room.

"Before we get to business, a word of advice," the Miracle Worker began. She removed her hat to reveal wavy hair of different shades of red, and she wore a dark purple bandana to keep it out of her face. "Next time someone you don't know calls you by name and announces that they know what you're looking for, turn the other way." She sat on a throne-like seat in front of her fireplace. "Strangers as informed as I am tend to have bad intentions."

"How did you know I wouldn't turn the other way?" Renée asked.

"I've been studying you for a very long time," the Miracle Worker explained. She played with the beads which decorated a couple of her twisted strands of hair. "And well, let's just say you're not the brightest person in the world. Now, have a seat and we'll discuss why you're here."

That same morning, Rein was in no hurry to catch up with the empress. If Renée felt like she could take care of herself, and if she knew where the Mystery Miracle Worker was located, she could find her on her own. Rein ate the last of her food along with a burdania petal, and then left the mushroom in search for a bird she could ride. She hoped this would be the last bird she would ever have to lasso. Catching and riding birds had become a tedious task and she was excited to not have to do it anymore.

It was a long flight to get to Incaendium. Luckily, it was easy to land her seagull there since the gravitational force on this island was the strongest in the world, and the bird most likely longed to rest. All the plant-life bent toward the ground and all the animals were a bit more lethargic, thus she was hardly in much danger of being hunted while she waited for the boarders of Roznova to explode into inferno. Finally, Rein saw the horizon glow and with some persuasion she urged the bird to take off. By the time she would reach Roznova, the flames would be gone and she would have ten minutes to find the home of the Mystery Miracle Worker.

Rein could feel the leftover heat of the fire surround her as she approached the island, and the steam from the boiling ocean rose up beneath her as she arrived. She believed she landed the bird on the part of the island where Captain Tzatara's map said the Mystery Miracle Worker's lair was located. After setting the bird free, she searched for the small hill while she repeated the description over and over again in her mind. Suddenly, the muscles in her left arm contracted in a spasm of agony. It stretched past her shoulder this time and reached around her throat like a groping fist. Rein knew what it was immediately and all she could do was wait for it to pass. She could swear that it lasted longer than the first time. Why did this aggravating reminder have to strike now when it was imperative she find the Mystery Miracle Worker's lair as soon as possible?

At long last, the pain of her oath subsided and before the ache had dissipated completely, Rein continued her desperate search for the small hill beside the glowflower bush. When she felt certain that her time was almost up, Rein spotted an area that displayed a willow tree, a glowflower bush, and a cluster of purple rocks among other plant-life; exactly what Captain Tzatara had explained was near to the entrance.

"That must be it," she told herself and she quickly leapt to the hill.

Rein peered behind the layers of moss and shrubbery when she heard a rustling that she knew she had not made. She paused and listened, but heard nothing more, so she continued to search beneath the moss for a small opening through which she could squeeze. Then she heard the sound again and she spun around with her knife drawn. She knew for a fact that something was there slowly moving toward her through the leaves and twigs; another distraction intent on stalling her. What could it be now?

Chapter Fourteen

This time the noise came from behind and goosebumps crawled along Rein's skin. She could swear that whatever it was rose tall above her head. She twirled around to make eye-contact with a king cobra as it towered over her. Before she could do or say anything, it snapped at her.

Rein bounded out of the way and slashed its face with her knife. The cobra hissed and attacked again. She pounced onto its head and tried to slide down its body while slicing it open on the way down but the cobra jolted and she fell off, losing her knife in the fall. The snake struck at her once more before she had the chance to get up, but she managed to roll away and jump to her feet. She drew her sword and waited for the cobra's next move. The cobra hissed and attacked her, but she dodged again and moved to stab it through the eye. The cobra avoided her blade and knocked the sword out of her hand with its tail.

Now Rein had no weapon. Her only means of defense were her agility and bare hands. She caught sight of her knife a couple feet to her right and bolted after it. She glanced over her shoulder for the cobra and evaded its next strike. Then she noticed it wrapping itself around her and she leapt over its scaly body. She snatched her knife back and faced the serpent just in time to slice its snout again, deeper this time. The cobra cried out in pain, however the cry sounded like it had a voice. This startled Rein.

"You can talk?" she asked.

"Yes," replied the cobra in a weary voice.

"Then why did you attack me?"

"Tell me, why are you here?" the cobra asked.

"I'm looking for the Mystery Miracle Worker."

"Exactly. I am protecting her."

"She's completely hidden from the world," Rein argued. "Why does she need protecting?"

"I will let her explain that to you herself," said the cobra. "You have defeated me, after all. Follow me."

Rein followed the cobra through the moss and into a hole between the giant rock and the entrance. Inside the cave, it was difficult to see anything, even with Rein's faint light. Fortunately, all she really needed to see was the cobra in front of her. They turned left once they approached the three other caves and then it wasn't long before she found herself beneath a lit torch. The snake disappeared into another hole in the wall and Rein followed.

They entered the Mystery Miracle Worker's lair where Rein found Empress Renée already consulting with the woman in front of a cute little fireplace to the left. It was a small and full room, though it appeared to be the perfect size for the Miracle Worker since it remained clean and organized. There was a bed in a corner to the right with hand-made pillows and fur blankets. Rein eyed the many books and strange-looking tools and devices, along with the various objects that people had used as trade for the Miracle Worker's assistance. One item that particularly stood out to Rein was a ship in a bottle that was placed on top of the bookcase. She had never seen anything so peculiar and seemingly pointless.

"Miss," said the cobra to the Miracle Worker. "I am wounded."

"Rein!" said Renée. "You made it!"

"No thanks to you!" Rein replied as she shook her sword at the empress. "I should prick you beneath your fingernails!"

The empress shied away from this remark and didn't reply.

"How are you wounded, Stephocra?" the Miracle Worker asked the cobra. Stephocra slithered over to the Miracle Worker who picked him up to examine him. "Oh my god! How did this happen?"

"I had a quarrel with a sprite creature," Stephocra answered.

"Is this the sprite creature?" the Miracle Worker asked, looking at Rein.

"I assure you it was in defense," said Rein. "I was only looking for you for help."

"I see," said the Miracle Worker. She carried Stephocra over to a long table surrounded by numerous candles. There she brought out a large magnifying glass to examine the cobra's wound closer. "Well you will have to wait your turn. First, I must tend to my guardian."

"If you don't mind me asking," said Rein as she climbed up the table leg. "Why do you have a guardian?"

"For the same reason I hid myself here," the Miracle Worker replied as she prepared the tools she would use on Stephocra. Rein took a seat on the lid of a round, porcelain tub. "I kept getting too many customers, a lot of them with nothing to trade. In most cases, I wouldn't mind, but I must make a living too. So, I decided to move to a place where only the most desperate customers with something to trade would find me. Then, the word of my location got out and I began getting those same customers, so I decided I needed a guardian." The Miracle Worker sighed. "Soon, I will be moving again. So let me guess why you are here: You want wings."

Rein raised her eyebrows. "How did you know?"

"Well clearly you're a pixie and you have no wings." The Miracle Worker applied ointment to Stephocra's wound. "I don't imagine you'd be here for much else."

"How is it clear that I'm a pixie?" Rein asked. "Few others can tell."

"Besides a full-sized fairy, pixies are the only creatures that produce their own natural light."

"Oh," said Rein. "I was sure there are other creatures that produce light."

"No," replied the Miracle Worker. She applied a small amount of some gooey substance to Stephocra's wound and used her tools to hold it shut. "You may be thinking of water and ice sprites, but they only capture light during the day and release it by night. They don't produce it. Additionally, their light is so dim, they might as well not have one. Only creatures of fairy descent produce light."

"Oh," said Rein. "So, no sprite is of fairy blood?"

"No, not even the ones that fly. Otherwise they would be called pixies and they would be the only blue-skinned fairies with identical wings. Notice that no two fairy wings are identical."

"Ah," said Rein. "I have a lot of sprite friends who won't be happy to hear that they aren't fairies."

"Then don't tell them," said Stephocra after the Miracle Worker released him. "They need not know."

"I wonder why the Fairy Circle hasn't clarified this," Rein wondered out loud.

"Probably because like Stephocra said, there's no reason for it." The Miracle Worker wiped her hands on a towel and addressed her cobra friend. "There you are. Now just go to your tree and take it easy for the rest of the day."

Stephocra slithered over to his leafless tree that stood next to the fireplace and perched himself in it.

"Did you find out what Renée is here for?" Rein asked.

"Yes I did," said the Miracle Worker as she cleaned up. "I think I'll help her last. As for you, what do you have to trade?"

"Excuse me." Empress Renée stood and approached the table. "Why should I be last?"

"Because your case is more complicated," the Miracle Worker answered.

"Well, here's the issue," Renée insisted. "I don't have much time."

"You can't spare a couple hours or less?" asked the Miracle Worker. "If you want what you came for and if you want every correct detail, you will let your pixie friend go first."

Renée heaved an impatient sigh. "Very well, but please be quick."

"Thank you." The Miracle Worker turned to Rein. "Now, what do you have to trade?"

"I have a couple things that may be of interest to you." Rein set down her pouch and sword in front of the Miracle Worker. "I have this sword that you might be able to make into a needle perhaps, or you can do something else with it. After I regain wings, I doubt I'll have much need for it. But my main source of trade is this pouch of burdania petals and seeds. There are twenty or so petals here. I'm not sure how many seeds, but there are a quite a bit. Pixies can't live long without wings, so we must eat a burdania petal once a day to stay alive. I'm sure you can do a lot with these."

"I've heard much about burdania flowers," Stephocra said. "That could be a very beneficial trade indeed."

The Miracle Worker gave it some thought before she finally said, "Let me explain what I can offer you before we agree on anything." She approached her bookcase and removed a wooden box which contained ten trays. "I have not yet had the fortune of discovering a way to induce the growth of wings in a pixie just yet, or in anything for that matter." She set the trays out in front of Rein for her to look them over. Each contained about sixteen sets of pixie wings. "However, I can offer you a single set and surgically place it into your back in such a way that you will fly again."

"Are these real pixie wings?" Rein asked. Curious, the empress glanced over them as well.

"Yes," replied the Miracle Worker as she strolled back to her bookcase to remove a large volume. "They were a form of payment to me long ago. The ogre-man explained it belonged to his great, great, great... great grandfather, who kept it as a collection once his pixie shop was closed down during the reign of King Plake."

"You're old enough to recall the era," said Stephocra.

"And the pixie shop," Rein added.

"This grandfather found a way to preserve the wings so that they wouldn't crystallize, which is why they are in such good condition," the Miracle Worker continued as she searched for a passage in the thick book. "You can even pinch them between your fingers and they won't fall apart. I tested them before I made the deal."

Rein tried not to pay attention to too much of what the Miracle Worker said. She was learning more than she wished to know and she wondered if it was all worth it. Did she want wings again so desperately that she would use a deceased pixie's wings?

"I can do this," she finally answered.

"Splendid," said the Miracle Worker. "Go ahead and choose the set that best fancies you. I think I might be able to use these flowers you brought me."

Rein tried not to think about how all these wings ended up in all these trays and forced herself to pay more attention to finding a set that best fit her personality. Of course, the empress pointed out her personal favorites, which turned out to be the designs which Rein liked the least. Once she got to the sixth case, her eyes landed on a simpler set with a spider web design. Her eyes grew round and a gasp caught in her throat.

"That set," Rein said pointing.

"Out of all these wings, you choose those?" the Miracle Worker asked after she put the book back on the shelf. "You haven't even finished looking."

"Yes," Rein answered. She swallowed hard. "Those are my original wings."

"Are they now?" said Stephocra, intrigued.

"Yes."

"Well, you lucky speck," said the Miracle Worker. "Let's get started then."

The Miracle Worker gently removed Rein's choice of wings from the tray and set them on a small strip of cotton. Then she replaced the trays back into the box and the box into the bookcase.

"How many times have you done this?" asked Empress Renée.

"Rein will be my fourth living wingless pixie," the Miracle Worker answered. She wiped the table down and cleaned the wings. "You all have very interesting stories concerning the loss of your wings, but I wouldn't expect anything less."

"Has it been successful each time?" the empress asked.

"Only the last two times. It's rare to be successful the first time around, I'm afraid. Fortunately for us, Rein chose an easy pair, so I expect her procedure to be a successful one."

"How's this going to work?" Rein asked.

"You're going to disrobe above the waist and lie face-down on this cotton ball here." The Miracle Worker set a cotton ball down on the table. "I'll give you something to eat that will make you a little woozy so you feel no pain, or at least not much. Then I'm going to open your back and attach your wings to the proper muscles as quickly as I can. After that we'll let you heal."

"Is the fact that the wings are crystallized going to be a problem?" Rein asked.

"No," the Miracle Worker answered as she set up a complicated magnifying contraption. She left the table for a moment. "Once they are attached to your muscles and the healing process begins, the wings will adjust themselves."

The Miracle Worker returned with a handful of tiny purple mushrooms with blue spots. Rein's stomach tightened with a mix of anticipation and panic, but she wanted her wings back so fiercely that she couldn't imagine anything she wouldn't do to obtain them. Nothing could get in her way at that point.

"You ready?" asked the Miracle Worker.

Rein sucked in a deep breath. "Yes."

Rein removed her coat and shirts and lay on the cotton ball like she had been instructed with her back facing the Miracle Worker. Then the Miracle Worker handed her a mushroom.

"Eat the entire thing slowly, and try to keep still."

Rein ripped off a handful of the mushroom and gnawed on it. Nearly two seconds after she had swallowed the first bite, she began to feel the effects.

"How's your vision?" the Miracle Worker asked.

"Fuzzy," Rein answered. "My head feels like it's inflating."

The Miracle Worker slowly sliced into Rein's back as she peered through the lens on her contraption. "Do you feel any pain?"

"No."

"Perfect. Continue to eat that mushroom until it's all gone. Meanwhile, why don't you share your story about how you lost your wings?"

By the time the Miracle Worker had finished the surgery, Rein was completely unconscious. After bandaging the pixie up, the Miracle Worker laid her on the mantelpiece to recover. Then she glanced at Empress Renée and returned to her table.

"Now, as for you," she said. "Firstly, I would advise you to hide that key a little better. You're practically asking for trouble by openly wearing it around your neck like a rhinestone."

"I didn't come here for fashion advice," Renée replied.

The Miracle Worker chuckled softly and began to clean her workplace. "Of course not. So why won't your pixie friend tell you where the Cataras Springs are?"

"All fairies have sworn an oath not to divulge such information."

The Miracle Worker squinted her eyes, curiously. "I see. You still have yet to offer me anything for such information."

"What do you want?"

"What do you have?"

"I have a lot. It would be easier if you told me what you want."

"Is that so?" asked the Miracle Worker as she casually cleaned her tools and put them away. "Well, I assume you're not going to give me the key. I suppose I'll have to come up with something else. In which case, I'll need time to consider. In the meantime, why don't you tell me what you want from the Cataras Springs?"

"That's none of your business," Renée said.

"You're not the empress here, woman!" Stephocra called from his tree. "For a smooth transaction, you'll do well to humble yourself."

The Miracle Worker smiled at her pet and then addressed Renée as she wiped down the table. "I could easily refuse you the location no matter what you offer me. There are plenty of other people who will be happy to get me whatever I please. So come now, *Your Majesty*. Humor me with some conversation."

Empress Renée paused for a moment and then reluctantly opted to give in. "I need the healing water for my daughter."

"Uh huh..." The Miracle Worker placed a cauldron on the table. "Do you like stag stew?"

"I've never had it before."

"Well you'll have some tonight." The Miracle Worker set a basket of freshly-cooked stag meat beside the cauldron and began shredding it. "I suggest you spend the night here. It'll take a while for me to decide what I want in return for the location, plus your pixie friend needs to recover."

"I told you before, I don't have much time."

"If you keep that key on display, it won't matter," said Stephocra.

"I'm sure you can spare one night," the Miracle Worker said as she sliced some vegetables with rapid skill. "The Cataras Springs aren't far, so there's no need to consider travel time."

"It's on this island?"

"Well, I didn't say that." The Miracle Worker mixed the vegetables into the cauldron with the meat and some water. "But you'll make the journey within a day should I decide to supply you its whereabouts. So you are safe to stay the night."

"Very well," Renée said.

It didn't appear Renée had much of a choice. What angered her most was how many orders she had taken during this entire journey even though *she* was the empress. If someone, *anyone*, could just spare the time to listen to her and take her seriously for once! So much time and trouble could have been saved if someone had genuinely considered her situation. But no, everyone had to make their own selfish needs priority.

The Miracle Worker added spices and herbs to the stew while Renée returned to her original seat by the fireplace. Finally, the Miracle Worker hung the cauldron over the fire.

"You thirsty?" she asked.

"I suppose I can drink something," Renée replied. "Whatever you have will do fine."

The Miracle Worker took her time preparing tea for them both and after setting the kettle over the fire, she sat in front of the impatient Empress Renée on her throne-like chair.

"So, Empress," the Miracle Worker began. "What do you know about the Cataras Springs?"

"Everything I need to know."

"Really? So then why do you still search for them?"

"I told you. I need the healing water for Nadia."

"Nadia being your adopted daughter," the Miracle Worker confirmed.

Renée felt her hackles rise but quickly brought herself under control. "Yes."

The Miracle Worker nodded her head, considering her next question. "How do you plan to bring this water to Nadia?"

"I can summon a bottle from the water in the air."

"Just any bottle created by yourself?" the Miracle Worker asked.

"Yes..."

The Miracle Worker couldn't help but smile.

"So, you in fact know *little* about the Springs," said Stephocra.

"What are you talking about?" Renée asked, her voice raised slightly.

"You don't think that the fairies would have *shown* you to the Cataras Springs if there was even the slightest chance it would help your situation, despite their oath?" the Miracle Worker asked. "Nadia is among the most worthy people to use the Springs and you're close friends with Queen Tiana. Yet, everyone has told you to forget about it."

"My *situation* is that I'm unhappy," said the empress. "The water from the healing spring will heal my daughter. Don't you think that will make me happy? And then... perhaps I can drink from the healing spring and it can heal my mind."

"Just your mind, Empress?" asked the Miracle Worker. "Nothing else?"

Empress Renée glanced shyly at the Miracle Worker. "Perhaps that too..."

The Miracle Worker tapped her nails against her armrest. "It is my understanding that seafolk aren't entirely informed about what makes nearly half of them infertile. Am I correct in this assumption?"

Renée eyed the Miracle Worker, intrigued. "You think you have the answers?"

"I've been doing my own research when I can," said the Miracle Worker. "I won't provide too many details since I don't know how much you can handle, but from what I can tell, many of those who are infertile are born without a womb."

Renée narrowed her eyes at the Miracle Worker. "Fascinating."

"My theory, following this discovery, is that this isn't a defect," the Miracle Worker explained further. "For seafolk, wombs are characteristics that some are born with and others are born without. Like hair color, the number of fins on their body, various abilities the may possess. If I'm correct, the healing spring won't help you, because there is nothing to heal."

Renée shuddered at these words, but fought desperately to hide her feelings. "Well, I suppose we'll find out soon enough, now won't we? I still plan to visit the Springs for Nadia's sake. So, do you know what it is you want in exchange for its location?"

The Miracle Worker shrugged and stood up from her seat. "No, I'm still trying to decide on that matter." She approached her cupboards where she removed two bowls and brought them back to the fireplace.

"I don't understand why it's so hard," Renée said. "You don't have much."

"We need not live like royalty to be happy," said Stephocra bluntly.

"Be nice, Stephocra," said the Miracle Worker. Then she addressed Renée while she stirred the stew in the cauldron. "Compared to what you're used to, I'm sure it doesn't appear to be much. However, I have quite a bit considering what I do for a living. If there's anything that I'm in need of, it would be items I can use for research and experiments."

"What exactly would those items be?"

The Miracle Worker scooped some of the stew into the bowls. "There are no specifics. Just some herb or plant, maybe a spice or specimen. Something you can offer that I think I can use, but don't imagine I could easily obtain. Like Rein's burdania seeds for instance." The Miracle Worker handed Renée a bowl and returned to her cupboards with the other one.

"I might be able to give you some plant from the ocean," Renée offered.

"Hmm," the Miracle Worker replied as she chopped a mushroom into tiny pieces. "I think I might have an idea, but let me ponder it. Perhaps I'll accept your offer instead."

The Miracle Worker searched her cabinets while Renée sighed and glanced around the cave. "So where am I to sleep?" she asked.

"There's a bed right there," replied the Miracle Worker as she pointed with an herb.

The empress turned to see the bed Rein had noticed when she had entered. It wasn't what she was used to sleeping on, but it was better than sleeping in a stone box like she had done for the past month.

"How long is it going to take for Rein to recover?" she asked.

"About four weeks," the Miracle Worker replied. She set a walnut shell filled with stew and extra herbs in front of Rein for her to eat when she returned to consciousness. She then took her seat, handed Renée a spoon, and ate from her own bowl of stew.

"That seems short," Renée commented.

"The last couple of times I did this procedure, it took each pixie about five weeks. But Rein seems to be in much better health than the other three, so I'd be surprised if she takes more than four weeks to recover."

"I see."

"Anyway, I've decided what I want from you if I'm to provide you with the location of the Cataras Springs."

"What?" Renée practically glowed.

"I want the key."

Chapter Fifteen

Empress Renée was confused. She furrowed her eyebrows and waited for an explanation from the Mystery Miracle Worker. However, she didn't get one.

"I thought we had already established that I won't give you the key," she said.

"Yes, and then I figured, 'what if she didn't need the key?'" the Miracle Worker replied. "You see, Empress, I know of an entrance into the Cataras Springs where you don't need a key. You can enter from beneath the island in which the garden is located."

Renée processed these words. "I still need the key to know how much time I have left."

"How does the key show you?" asked the Miracle Worker. She held out her hand to receive the key.

The empress hesitated, but handed the key over. "When the rose has completely bloomed, my time is up."

The Miracle Worker examined the key. "How long ago did you receive it?"

"About a year and seven months ago I think," Renée answered.

"At what stage was the rose?"

"It was a bud barely opening."

The Miracle Worker calculated for a moment and then handed the key back to the empress. "You have just under five weeks left."

"How can you be so sure?" Renée asked.

"Estimation based on calculation," the Miracle Worker answered. "Just take my word for it. You have approximately four weeks, maybe a couple of days more left."

"She's pure human," Stephocra explained further. "Statistically, humans are more knowledgeable than other ethnicities. She's more likely to provide you with an accurate estimate."

"True, but they are also more emotional than most," Renée replied. "Perhaps she's desperate for the key."

"What does it matter if you don't need it anymore?" the Miracle Worker asked. "I have another way for you to enter the Springs which doesn't require the key, and you'll be there the very same day you leave Roznova."

Renée considered. "You said it's on an island. Do you mean one of the Continent Islands?"

"Yes," said the Miracle Worker. "If you give me the key, I'll tell you how to enter the Springs from beneath the island. It's much easier and it'll save you time. You'll even have time to wait for Rein to finish recovering. How does that sound?"

It was clear that Renée considered the offer. The Miracle Worker had no reason to keep her from saving

Nadia, what would she gain from that? Surely this offer was true and beneficial to them both.

"Are you sure it's easier and faster?" she asked.

"I'm positive."

Renée took a while longer to consider before she finally handed over the key.

"Wonderful," said the Miracle Worker as she took the key. She dropped it down her purple blouse before she continued speaking. "Now, you must pay close attention. It's only fast and easy when you remember every little detail."

"I'm listening," Renée replied.

"Do you know where Carnific is?" the Miracle Worker asked as she set her stew down on her end table.

"No."

"Very well, I'll show you later, but the Cataras Springs are in the core of the island. Once you arrive at Carnific, look for the underwater entrance to the island. It will be the biggest cave you find. It's very large and rocky inside, so it's easy to get lost. Continue straight until you reach the volcanoes and, I suppose you can call them, 'ice chambers.' They're… rooms that are completely frozen. After the first few chambers, there will be an opening (maybe more than one), which will not be an ice chamber or contain an underwater volcano. Turn right at the first opening. You'll see bubbles containing different sea creatures that seem to decorate the area. That is how you'll know you're in the right place. Continue onward. It will get darker before it gets lighter. From what I've heard, a lot of sirens live there.

I haven't heard good things about sirens, but it may be different for you. I thought I'd warn you just in case.

"Anyway, you will eventually see an extinct creature frozen into the wall. I couldn't tell you what such a creature is, the sprite who told me all this said he forgot the name of it. He assured me it's quite clear when you've reached it. Turn left when you see this creature. You will be surrounded by clouds of color, but you shouldn't have a problem with them. They're just a bunch of acids, but since you're made of water, you should be fine. So just continue to the end and you will find yourself in a large room where it will appear as though beams of color are shooting down from the ceiling. Ascend through the dark blue beam. That's when you'll have entered the springs."

Renée did her best to archive everything the Miracle Worker said. "How did you memorize all of that?" she asked.

"The sprite wrote it down for me in return for a miracle. I memorized it and burned the paper. That way no one could steal it from me."

"How do I know that everything you just told me is true?"

"Sometime after I burned the paper, I had a fairy confirm everything for me. So I guarantee you, everything I told you is accurate. That's all I have to offer in terms of proof."

"How many fairies come through here?"

"More than you'd think," Stephocra answered.

"They mainly come to me for advice," the Miracle Worker added as she lifted her bowl of stew off the table to continue eating. "Since obviously they're able to help each other with most illnesses and losses."

"I see," Renée replied. Clearly Queen Tiana had lied to her about Aranel being the only fairy to know the location of the Mystery Miracle Worker. But it didn't matter right then. "Do you think you can write everything down again for me?"

"Yes, but you won't be able to take it with you since my paper will dissolve in water."

"Then while I wait for Rein to recover, I'll memorize it."

"Works for me. I'll write it down once I've finished eating."

While the Mystery Miracle Worker nursed Rein back to health for the next few weeks, the empress strived to memorize every detail involving the entrance into the Cataras Springs from beneath the ocean, but it wasn't working out for her. She managed to remember some things, but not the most important pieces of information. She grew frustrated, which only made memorization more difficult to achieve. Upon the advice of the Mystery Miracle Worker, she took a break and then worked to memorize only the important details. The Miracle Worker aided with pop quizzes every once in a while as well. This method seemed to work better.

When Rein no longer had to consume the purple mushrooms and their effects began to fade, the fog began to clear from her mind and she found it difficult to remember anything that had happened since the underground lair. All she could recall were missed-matched events that had taken place in the White Castle and as far as she knew, that's where she had awakened. She needed to find the empress. She needed to save her! They needed to find the Mystery Miracle Worker! She pushed herself up from the cotton ball in a frenzied panic and a scream grew within her chest.

"Relax, Rein," said the Miracle Worker. "You're safe. Your memory will return soon. Take a moment to gather your surroundings. You'll connect the dots before you know it."

Immediately after the Mystery Miracle Worker spoke, everything began to make sense again and Rein calmed down as she reviewed her returned memories. She glanced around the room and spotted the empress on the bed studying a piece of paper.

"What's she doing?" Rein asked the Miracle Worker.

"She's memorizing how to enter the Cataras Springs without the key," answered Stephocra, who was wrapped around the Miracle Worker's bicep.

Rein searched her memory vigorously. What were the Cataras Springs? Why has this subject entered the conversation? How does one enter the Springs without a key? She removed her left glove and examined the glowing scar on her palm. It all came back to her in a matter of seconds.

"How did you know about that entrance?" Rein asked the Miracle Worker.

"A sprite told me in exchange for a miracle."

"Might I see the paper?"

"Ask the empress." The Miracle Worker walked away and prepped a kettle for tea.

"Renée, may I see that paper?" Rein asked.

The empress sighed and approached Rein with the sheet of parchment. "I suppose I need a break anyway. Can you read Northern Elvish?"

"Of course, it's the most common Elvish," Rein answered as she took the page.

"Very well. How are you feeling?"

"Confused," said Rein. "Tired. I'm sure I'll feel better soon."

Rein carefully read the words on the page and was very disturbed about how much information regarding the Cataras Springs had gotten out to the world.

"He gave you legitimate, detailed directions!" Rein said.

"He needed a miracle, I needed the details," the Miracle Worker replied. "In the end, it worked out for everyone."

Rein continued to find herself more and more astonished as she learned exactly how many people were close to entering the Cataras Springs. If so many people had such detailed information, she could expect that some probably knew how to find the more dangerous springs inside the garden. This only made matters worse. Then she remembered that it had been over four hundred years since the Springs had been created; fairykind should be pleased that it had all remained a secret for this long. Hopefully, after she showed Captain Tzatara the Springs, the Fairy Circle wouldn't hesitate to destroy them.

"May I have it back now?" the empress asked Rein.

"Sure," Rein replied. "But why are you studying that when you have the key?"

"I told her I would tell her the faster and easier way to enter the Springs if she gave me the key," the Miracle Worker replied for the empress. "I also told her how much time she has left, so she no longer needs the key. Now, let me check your back and see how the wings are healing."

Before Rein had time to reply, the Miracle Worker laid her on another cotton ball on the table and cut the bandages off to reveal her wings. She used a soft cloth to wipe the dried blood and other fluids away to get a better view of the progress.

While she did this, Rein reviewed everything she had just learned. The Miracle Worker now had the key and seemed to know everything there was to know about the Cataras Springs. What did she want with the Springs? How could Rein get the key back? *Could* she get the key back? In order to do so, she would have to know where the Miracle Worker had hidden it. But she couldn't simply ask where it was and she probably wouldn't have the chance to search around the lair.

"Just as I thought," commented the Miracle Worker.

"Is that good?" Rein asked.

"It's very good," said Stephocra.

"You are almost completely healed and the wings are in a normal, healthy condition," the Miracle Worker explained. "Let's see if they work. Raise them, *slowly*." Rein obeyed. "Do you feel any discomfort or pain?"

"It just feels weird. I'm so used to not having wings."

"I can imagine. Try hovering now." Rein obeyed and then dropped back onto her feet. "Pain or discomfort?"

"Just some strain."

"That's normal considering you haven't used these muscles for some time. Try flying around the room a little."

Rein fluttered about for a moment and then returned to the table. "No pain," she said. "It is a little tiring."

"It will be for some time," said the Miracle Worker. "You'll have to use those muscles often before you can become your normal self again. A diet of nuts and oats should help to strengthen those muscles."

"Nuts and oats," Rein repeated. "I'll keep that in mind."

"Just don't do too much flying for the first couple of days. Perhaps use whatever method of travel you have been using lately to get to Carnific."

"Will do."

The Miracle Worker handed Rein her coat and shirts and Rein redressed herself. She flapped her wings a little bit and smiled. Finally, she had wings again! It was all she could do to withhold her screams of joy.

The Miracle Worker cleaned up her work area once more as she said, "You two are set to leave whenever you wish. My work with you is complete."

Empress Renée approached the table and returned the sheet of parchment to the Miracle Worker. "Thank you," she said. "I think I can remember all the important details at this point." She turned to Rein. "Meet you there?"

"Sounds good to me," Rein said, glowing. She waited for Renée to leave and then turned to the Miracle Worker who burned the page with a candle. "So, she's actually going to the Springs then?"

"Yes, I tried to talk her out of it as I'm sure you have," the Miracle Worker replied as she sprinkled some herbs into the kettle for her tea. "Have you told her why the Springs won't help her?"

"I tried to," said Rein. "But after her conversation with Tiana, Renée thinks we're all just trying to protect the Springs."

"Interesting." The Miracle Worker faced Rein. "Did you tell Renée about your oath?"

"What do you know of my oath?" Rein narrowed her eyes at the Miracle Worker and tucked her left hand behind her back.

"Nothing, actually. But I imagine it has something to do with any of the wonders the Fairy Circle created. I'm willing to bet the Cataras Springs. Sharing it with the empress may have proved that you aren't all that concerned about protecting them."

"I doubt it, honestly," Rein replied. "I don't think anything could convince Renée at this point. I think I was too late and she was dead set when I spoke with her."

"So it does have something to do with the Cataras Springs then," the Miracle Worker confirmed.

"I didn't reveal the location, if that's what you're thinking. I only promised to let him inside if he gave me your location so that I can get wings again; he figured the rest out on his own."

"Ah, so how did you plan to let him inside if Renée decided to give up her pursuit for the Springs? It's not as though you were going to take the key after her time was up since, as I've been told, that's when the Fairy Circle plans to destroy the Springs."

"Yes but…" Rein came upon a realization.

"Is it safe to say you *wanted* Renée to arrive at the Springs?" the Miracle Worker asked. "You needed to make this oath to regain wings and you need her at the Springs with the key in order to keep your oath. It appears to me that you may have put some effort into convincing the empress not to pursue the Springs for Nadia's sake, but not as much effort as you could have for your sake."

Rein ran the Miracle Worker's words through her head and could find no objection to them. She was right. Rein didn't try as hard as she could have to convince the empress, and the reason was because of her oath to Captain Tzatara. And now Nadia was going to be cursed and banished to land because of it. She had to redeem herself.

"I gotta go," Rein breathed. "Please tell me you plan to enter the Cataras Springs with the key soon."

The Miracle Worker tapped her thumb on the counter. "As soon as possible."

Rein had to accept this answer. It was better than a "no." She darted out of the Mystery Miracle Worker's lair and then out of the cave. Already she experienced issues with her wings. Maneuvering about was a challenge and then when she perched in a tree, her muscles ached. Unfortunately, she had little faith that she would find a bird on this island and knew that she would most likely have to fly all the way to Incaendium to hunt a bird there. Once again, pain shot up her arm and this time it claimed the entire left side of her torso.

"I know, I *know*!" Rein screamed. "I'll figure something out, I swear! Please, stop!"

Once the pain decreased to a throbbing ache, Rein took off to fly to the neighboring island where she dropped to the branch of a tree, panting madly. There would be no more flying for a while after that trip. She was almost concerned that she had damaged something based on the immense soreness between her shoulder blades. With much struggle, Rein managed to lasso herself a seagull and began her journey to Carnific, which was two more islands away in the direction of Arcor.

Rein and Renée had unknowingly passed the same mysterious cloaked man who had been following them since Arcor. He had hidden in the darkness of the cave for the entire time the two of them consulted with the Mystery Miracle Worker. After Rein left, the man entered the room and stood in the doorway, waiting for the Miracle Worker to notice his presence.

"He emerges at last," she said without looking at him. "I wondered how long you would loom in the darkness outside my lair."

Chapter Sixteen

The Mystery Miracle Worker removed two copper cups from her cupboard and set them on the counter. Meanwhile, the mysterious man took a seat in front of the fireplace and never removed his hood to show his face.

"You knew I was here all along," he said. "And here I thought you would be surprised to see me again."

"The only thing that surprises me is that you stayed for so long," replied the Miracle Worker. "I thought you would surely leave after I convinced my last clients to stay. You must really want what you came for."

"Indeed, I do."

"So, what is it?" the Miracle Worker asked, turning to face him. "My instructions failed you?"

"You remember everything, don't you?"

"How could we forget?" asked Stephocra.

"I even remember your name," the Miracle Worker added. "Ravan of Rivas, the customer surely up to no good."

"What I'm up to is none of your business." Ravan laced his fingers together.

"Did you miss our conversation with the empress?" asked Stephocra.

"It doesn't matter," said the Miracle Worker. "I've always had enough of an idea as to what he's been up to."

"Then why do you help me? It appears you know many people who are after the same thing, and clearly you're one of them."

"True, but most will fail to find it," Stephocra said.

"So tell me why you've returned," said the Miracle Worker. "I'm assuming you didn't find her."

"Oh, I found her," Ravan replied. "And I got what I needed from her. I'm here because I need the directions from you."

"I only have directions from beneath the ocean."

"Don't insult me," said Ravan. "I may not be pure human, but I'm certainly no fool. You have the directions from land and you have them memorized."

"Even if I do, I know there's no chance that you're going to expose what you received from the nymph, so you're not going to get it. I'm afraid you're wasting your time with me." The Miracle Worker turned to finish preparing her tea.

"There must be something else you wish for," Ravan pried.

"Not from you," Stephocra answered.

Ravan stood and began to exit. "It seems as though today I won't be breaking you. But we both know that only I can get you absolutely anything you need or want, no matter the risk. Don't forget that."

The Miracle Worker shot a glance at Stephocra and they smirked at each other. It seemed as though everything was going exactly the way they wanted it to.

"Ravan," called the Miracle Worker. He stopped at the entrance and she leaned against her counter. "Why don't you have a seat here and perhaps we can work something out. There's no sense in bartering like a couple of Arcorian thieves; as a human I prefer to do business in a more civilized manner." She poured them both some tea and they each took a seat across from each other at the table. "So, let's start with a little conversation."

Ravan eyed the cup in front of him. "You first."

"Very well," replied the Miracle Worker as she sat back in her chair. "You mentioned that you could get me absolutely anything I—"

"No, Sweetheart," Ravan interrupted. "The tea. You first."

The Miracle Worker looked at the pot and then her cup. "You think I poisoned it?"

"Why not?"

"For the same reason I asked you to stay. You're right, I could use you."

"Very good... you first."

"Very well." The Miracle Worker took a drink of her tea.

"The whole cup, please."

The Miracle Worker rolled her eyes, downed the cup of cinnamon and mint tea, and set it upside down on the table. "Satisfied?"

Ravan took a sip of his tea and the Miracle Worker poured herself another cup.

"For your information, if I were to poison you, I would use something I'm immune to. So much for being no fool."

Slowly, Ravan set his cup down and examined her and Stephocra, searching for confirmation that he truly did ingest a poison.

"However, the fact remains that you're quite useful," the Miracle Worker continued. "So, in the future, I advise that you don't eat or drink anything offered by anyone. For your sake and mine."

"Noted." Ravan lifted the cup from the table again. "So, you were saying?"

"Yes, I was. You mentioned you could get me anything I need. Tell me, exactly how much is 'anything?'"

"Exactly what 'anything' means, Sweetheart," Ravan answered. "What is it you need?"

"Well actually, there is an issue. You see, there are many things that I need and want, and yes, you are the only one who can obtain them for me at this time. But the problem is that now is not the time to retrieve them, and I'm not sure which I will need first."

"That is a problem. So did you have a solution?"

"First things first. I require some confirmation. I told you my little secret, now you tell me yours. What do you seek in the Springs, and do you know how to find it?"

Ravan paused, contemplating. He remained motionless, the hood of his cloak still casting a shadow over his face so that neither the Miracle Worker nor her cobra friend could read his thoughts. Finally he answered, "I seek the Spring of Power. I do know how to find it, but I'm not going to tell you so much."

"Fair enough," the Miracle Worker replied casually. "I don't seek power from the Springs anyway. But why is that the fountain you seek? Do you wish to take over a kingdom? The world, perhaps?"

"That's way too much responsibility. I want something far simpler, but almost as grand. I wish to be a *better* miracle worker. I want kings and queens to come to me for miracles, potions, help in general—"

"Advice?"

"I cannot advise someone on how to rule. If I had such advice, I'd wish to rule."

"I see. I think you've confirmed everything I needed." The Miracle Worker stood up and approached her desk where she removed two large sheets of parchment, a quill, and an ink well before she sat back down. "So here's my solution. I will tell you where the Springs are. That is all I will tell you. You'll have to figure everything else out on your own. In return, you will be in debt to me. Like I said, I need nothing from you right now, but I will in the future. When that time comes, you will not refuse to give me what I want. It is all written in this contract. Now the question is, do you agree to my terms?"

Ravan continued to sit unnervingly still for a moment as he processed the offer. Soon, the only movement he made was to lift the parchment from the table to read over the contract… the contract which the Miracle Worker had already had prepared for some suspicious reason. The air was tense as the Miracle Worker and her cobra friend waited for Ravan to speak.

"Is there a list of things that you may want that I can, perhaps, look over before I agree to this?" Ravan finally asked as he set the contract back down.

"No. You'll just have to trust me that it will in no way affect you and whatever your status may be in the future, so long as you still have the power you plan to possess after your trip to the Springs."

Ravan considered one last time. "Very well. I accept your terms."

"Then you will sign at the bottom." The Miracle Worker handed Ravan a crimson quill.

"There's no ink in the well," Ravan said.

"Patience," Stephocra replied.

The Miracle Worker suddenly produced a dagger from her long, burgundy sleeve, snatched Ravan's wrist, and sliced into his palm before he had time to react. Ravan sat there in shock as he slowly bled into the ink well.

"You will sign with your blood," the Miracle Worker explained simply.

"What will this guarantee?"

The Miracle Worker grinned at her client. "I put a truth serum in the tea." Then she sat back down and handed Ravan a handkerchief to stopper the wound. "It is flowing through both our veins at this very moment and has infected our blood. Not only does this confirm that we have been honest with each other, but it also means that you cannot possibly break this contract. Now, sign at the bottom or you will not receive what you came for."

Ravan held the handkerchief against his wounded hand and hesitated. "Didn't you say a moment ago that you would poison me with a venom you're immune to?"

"Yes, a venom," the Miracle Worker answered. "Truth serum is not a venom. It's a serum."

"One cannot be immune to serum," Stephocra clarified.

"Trust me, I've tried," added the Miracle Worker. "Now sign."

Ravan finally gave in and signed on the dotted line with his own blood. Then the Miracle Worker took back the contract and the quill and examined the signature.

"Wonderful," she said. "And don't worry, the serum will eventually fade. It only remains permanent in the blood outside the body. And since it will always be in this bloody signature of *yours*, our terms can never be broken."

The Miracle Worker set the contract aside and began to draw a map complete with a compass on the second sheet of parchment. She still used Ravan's blood as ink, which made him a bit uneasy. Luckily for him, the hood of his silver cloak hid this feeling entirely.

"The Springs are hard to miss when you know what you're looking for," the Miracle Worker explained. Ravan wrapped the handkerchief around his palm as he listened. "This is a map of Carnific. You want to go to here." She marked a specific spot on the island and scribbled measurements to aid in the exact location. "You'll observe a large area of nothing but grass. Look among the trees circling this area. You should find a tree that reflects everything around it, but not you. That's how you'll know you're in the right place. However, the Cataras Springs are located deep beneath this spot. You'll have to figure out how to enter on your own."

"Don't worry, Sweetheart," Ravan said as he took the map. "I have a way. That's why I'm not after that key."

"Yet you arrived at the exact same time as the empress who had the key, which leaves me to believe you were following her. Why?"

"I needed to be in the presence of your key for at least a week. It gives the piece I have the power it needs to enter the Springs. But since I kept missing your client, I was unable to do that until recently. You just gave me that much needed time for free." Ravan stood up to leave. "Thank you for your business."

"Thank you for yours," the Miracle Worker said.

She and Stephocra watched Ravan exit the lair and waited a few seconds before anything else was said.

"He has the other key to the Springs?" Stephocra asked.

"He certainly does," she answered. "He has the dagger."

"The circle of fairies is not thrilled right now."

"Indeed," said the Mystery Miracle Worker. A smile stretched across her face as she glanced at the signature on the contract. "But I am."

Chapter Seventeen

Rein couldn't find any sign of Renée as she made her way to Carnific, so she decided to wait until the empress arrived inside the Cataras Springs. She landed in a tree on the island after about three hours of non-stop flight and scanned the jungle-life around her to make sure she was in the right place before she set the seagull free.

Rein opened a hidden hatch in the tree, jumped inside, and slid a long distance deep into the island. It had been a while since she last visited the Cataras Springs, so this dark tumble into the underground made her nerves a bit flustered. She soared out of an uprooted tree root and safely caught herself in the air. She glanced around to verify her location and then flew toward a small mushroom town deep in the garden. There, she approached a specific lavender mushroom home next to a sparkling blue stream and she knocked on the tiny wooden door. A brown-haired pixie dressed similarly to Rein opened the door and glowed at the sight of her.

"Rein Bow!" she exclaimed.

"Lilli Padd," Rein replied pushing her back inside. She shut the door before she continued. "There's no time for hellos. Someone's coming to the Springs. Many, actually."

"Really?" Lilli asked. "Who?"

"Empress Renée of the five oceans, some pirates, and perhaps the Mystery Miracle Worker."

"Why are so many people coming all at once?" asked Lilli. "And how do you know about it?"

Rein answered Lilli speaking at a hundred miles per hour and Lilli hardly caught anything she said. When Rein had finished telling her story, she added, "We need to move everyone out of here right now. They'll be arriving soon."

"What's the problem?" asked a darkly-dressed male pixie who had just entered the home.

"Rein Bow just reported that we're getting some questionable visitors," Lilli answered. "Start spreading the news and tell everyone to pack their belongings."

"Plural, huh?" He looked Rein up and down. "And you expect us to believe you didn't lead at least one of them here?"

"Relax, Thundre Storm," said Lilli.

"I bet that's how you got your wings back," he continued. Rein narrowed her eyes at him. "You do realize that this is the only home the merpixies have and you just took it from them, right?"

"Enough," Lilli said in Rein's defense. "We both know that there were many before her who gave them the majority of the information they have. For all we know, you may be one of those who are more responsible."

"Fine, but if you haven't noticed, she swore an oath," Thundre pointed out. Rein glanced at her hand where the glow shown through the glove.

"She told me," Lilli said. "Just leave."

Thundre glared at Rein before he exited the mushroom without another word.

"I'm sorry," Rein said with her head bowed.

Lilli sighed. "It doesn't matter. We all knew this day was going to come sooner or later, with or without help from anyone else. I'll make sure everyone gets the news. Why don't you keep watch for the pirates and the Mystery Miracle Worker with the rest of the lookouts?"

Rein exited the mushroom to find a group of pixies standing around brooding, shooting daggers at her, and Thundre was among them. Rein glared back at them but didn't utter a word. Nothing she could say would make them side with her. So she flew off and exited the Springs through the same tree by which she had entered. She sat on a limb and looked over the ocean to wait to see sails or a rowboat appear on the horizon. As she waited, she removed her glove to observe the scar on her palm, which ached consistently at this point. It shined brightly enough to hurt her eyes. After three centuries of longing to gain something, Rein now found herself longing to be rid of something.

Empress Renée drew near to the island from the ocean and her viewpoint was almost as beautiful as Rein's aerial view. The roots of the larger trees stretched far out into the water and arched over the surface to create a scenic route for those approaching Carnific by ship. Renée advanced closer to the island and searched for the entrance the Mystery Miracle Worker informed her about. Meanwhile she ran the description through her mind, hoping beyond hope that she remembered the directions correctly. She eventually found the entrance in the darkest shadows of the island and entered a bit hesitantly.

Once she was inside this grotto, Renée noticed it was exactly what the Miracle Worker said it would be: dark and extensive, with pillars of rock descending from the ceiling and ascending from the abyss below. It was definitely easy to get lost in there. However, Renée also found it easy to become distracted by its immense beauty. Flowery tree roots extended from the walls, the ceiling, and the pillars. Beams of light shot diagonally throughout the grotto, seemingly from out of nowhere. Then the sinister sound of siren song surrounded Renée as their words bounced off the walls and pillars. It snagged her attention away from the décor and her calm state of mind faded all too quickly. Her sudden spike of adrenaline and anxiety affected her memory and she realized that she had forgotten what she needed to do next. She felt that the best idea would be to simply move forward, deeper into the island while she fought to recall her next step.

As Renée continued into the cave, numerous tall underwater volcanoes came into view on her left. Lava oozed out the top of each one of them and flowed down their bodies. Renée was never able to catch sight of the ocean floor, even with the glowing magma seeping toward it. She glanced to her right and saw the "ice chambers" that the Mystery Miracle Worker had mentioned. The pillars were frosted and crystal designs etched up and down the walls. They reminded Renée that she would soon have to turn right, so she inched closer to the chambers. Suddenly, she felt a painful frost strike her right arm. She panicked and looked to find her arm completely frozen solid and she scrambled away from the chamber in a mad frenzy. Then her stomach dropped as her arm disconnected from her torso and plummeted into the abyss beneath her.

Empress Renée's apprehension hit a dramatic peak and she almost went completely insane. She felt the need to remain as quiet as possible, so instead of shrieking in horror, she hyperventilated and whimpered with her only remaining hand covering her mouth. She hovered there between the volcanoes and ice chambers, and strived to keep calm. The healing spring. The healing spring can give her another arm. Yes, she will arrive to the Cataras Springs and drink from the healing waters. This thought steadily lowered her blood pressure and after a few more calming breaths, Renée forced herself to continue with her remaining fist clenched.

Renée turned right as she was meant to, and her surroundings confirmed she was headed in the correct direction. The walls were spotted with bubbles, which seemed to generate their own light to illuminate the cavern.

Like the Mystery Miracle Worker had promised, they all contained some form of sea creature, each of them eyeing the empress intently. Renée hardly noticed them due to her intense episode of shock, and once again she forgot the next step. She leaned against a wall to take a moment to think and accidentally popped one of the bubbles, which allowed for a fanged stingray to escape. Even though it couldn't do much damage to a naiad, it frightened her and she shot ahead. She turned right again when she got the chance, but unfortunately, she was supposed to go left.

Moss hung down from the ceiling of the room Renée had entered and she noticed the presence of sirens. The sirens paused in the middle of their chorus to acknowledge their guest and slowly began to encircle her. The existence of sirens in these caverns explained the frozen chambers and the icy climate, as sirens lived in the coldest of waters. They appeared as transparent mermaids, all female, and they were a species so distinct from any other creature that it was easy to tell what they were. One could go as far to say that they were the fairies of the ocean in a sense, as they lived long without the need for reproduction; except these creatures weren't as nice as fairies.

"Your Majesty!" they exclaimed in their sweet, soft voices. "You're here!"

"Welcome!"

"What brings you here?"

"We're so excited to see you!"

"Come with us!"

"We'll have a tea party!"

They all led Renée in the complete opposite direction of where she needed to go, but Renée was still too dazed to object. Their soft laughter filled the room and their words cooed the empress into subservience.

"Oh, Your Majesty!" they continued as they dragged her farther along. "You lost your arm!"

"Your arm is gone!"

"How did this happen?"

"We must fix this."

"Hide in here!"

"We'll go find your arm."

They tossed Renée into a hollow and froze up the opening. Then they began to celebrate and only then did Renée fully understand her situation.

"Go tell the emperor we have his wife hostage," said one siren to the others.

"Wait!" Renée called. "What's the meaning of this? Let me out of here!" The siren giving the orders simply smiled at Renée and swam off. "I'll demand your complete genocide when I get out of here!"

The last threat was futile, as not only had all the sirens gone, but they wouldn't have let her out anyway. All that the empress could do now was either sit and wait for someone to free her, or to devise an escape plan of her own. She tried to kick the iced doorway out with all her might, but that didn't seem to do any good at all. Renée came to the conclusion that she was stuck there until someone else came to her aid. At this rate, she was never going to make it to the Cataras Springs, she was never going to replace her arm, she was never going to be happy, and she was never going to bear children. Oh, and most importantly, she was never going to save Nadia.

Chapter Eighteen

Not long after Ravan had left Roznova, the Mystery Miracle Worker packed a small bag of food for herself and a couple of oddly shaped, multi-colored, glass bottles. She wrapped the bottles in a thick, soft cloth and tightly packed them in her satchel to make sure that they were kept safe. Then she put on her large-brimmed hat, threw a gray shawl over her shoulders, and turned to her king cobra who was perched in his tree.

"Are you ready, Stephocra?"

"I couldn't be more ready, Miss," Stephocra replied as he slithered up her arm.

The Miracle Worker put out all the lights in her lair and raced to a dinghy she kept some distance from the beach, her burgundy skirts catching and tearing on foliage along the way. She had covered the boat with damp moss to hide it from any visitors and to prevent it from catching fire. As she uncovered it, she kept a wary eye out for Ravan. She didn't fully trust that he had the dagger to the Cataras Springs and believed there was a chance he was waiting around for an opportunity to take the key from her. She tossed her satchel into the dinghy before pushing it to the beach. There wasn't much time to waste as she imagined she only had a little over five minutes remaining before the ring of fire erupted again. She thrust the boat far out to the ocean and took care to spend little time in the hot water, even though her leather boots were coated to protect her feet from the heat. Finally, she hopped inside and rowed vigorously. It took every minute of the time she had left to scull far enough away from the disaster area, but when she had made it, she relaxed a little and took her time rowing through the smoke and boiling water to Carnific.

After waiting for what felt like hours, Rein spotted a large ship with dark gray sails on the horizon slowly making its way to the island. Rein forced herself to be patient. By the end of the day her oath would be fulfilled and the bonds would be broken. She simply had to wait just a short while longer.

Meanwhile, Captain Tzatara peered at the island through his telescope. Carnific looked like a thick jungle island beyond the broad roots bending over the waves, but as every island on the Continent Islands chain, it held a dangerous secret. Fortunately, the captain was well aware of this secret, and he possessed not a care in the world.

"That be it, gents!" he announced to his crew. "Now remember to bring yer own water and rum. The water source on the island be no good. Make ready the longboat!"

"Aye, Cap'n!"

Captain Tzatara took five of his able-bodied men, including his first mate, and rowed to the shore. Rein didn't feel like making her presence known just yet. She simply followed the gang from a distance as they hiked through the dense vegetation toward the Cataras Springs. The men were careful not to touch the streams, ponds, and other sources of water that they came across. Some were even so cautious to use swords and dry sticks to move the vegetation out of their path.

Soon, they came across a rushing river where they found the headless skeletal remains of a deer lying beside it. Shortly after, a doe came into view. Everyone watched as she glanced around and lightly sniffed the air. Then she stepped into the river where immediately, her leg sizzled and she released an ear-piercing cry of unexpected agony before collapsing into the stream. The water which rushed over her dissolved her body in waves of brown and crimson. The pirates watched the spectacle in silent astonishment, but their captain forced them to continue onward as if unmoved.

As the Mystery Miracle Worker approached Carnific, she and Stephocra spotted the pirate ship, and she didn't seem surprised.

"It appears we have competition, Miss," said Stephocra.

"Fortunately, I'm the one with the key," the Miracle Worker replied. "I wonder if they're working with Ravan."

"He doesn't seem the type to work with a team," Stephocra commented.

"I agree. Which makes me wonder how they plan to enter. Unless they're the ones to whom the pixie made her oath."

The Miracle Worker stepped out of her dinghy and dragged it onto shore before she began her own hike to the Cataras Springs. With Stephocra wrapped around her forearm, she passed by the streams and creeks without worry and she didn't give the dead animals by the river a second look. However, she kept a sharp eye out for Ravan as she felt he wasn't too far away.

The Miracle Worker slowed her pace at the sound of voices ahead. She and Stephocra peered from behind a tree and squinted to see who was there. Since they could see nothing, they continued forward cautiously, looking intently for whom they were following behind. Then, about a yard or so ahead of them, the Miracle Worker and Stephocra caught sight of Captain Tzatara and his band of thieves in an empty patch of forest. They waited there in silence and watched as Rein appeared from the mirror-tree she had mentioned to Ravan. The captain and his pirates spotted her too.

"There ya are!" exclaimed Captain Tzatara. "We've been waiting for ya."

"I know you have," Rein replied. "I've been trying to get the inhabitants of the Springs out before anyone came in."

"That's fine," the captain said, not particularly caring. "Where be the key?"

Rein took a deep breath before answering. "Someone else has it."

Meanwhile, Empress Renée remained trapped in the icy hollow of the cavern, still hopeless about ever making it to the Cataras Springs. She had been digging at the side of the frozen wall with a shell, just for something to do while she waited for the sirens to return. Then, she noticed something that made her melancholy heart jump in excitement. She had dug to the bottom of the frozen wall! Renée continued to dig harder and faster until she was sure she had enough room to flow out of the hollow like a current.

Renée did her best to remain quiet once she was out and she rushed back to the corridor that was decorated with bubbles. Once she arrived she searched madly for the frozen extinct creature while also trying to remain hidden from any sirens who might have stayed behind. She finally found the frightening frozen figure; a mammoth starfish whose mouth alone was the size of Renée herself. She could examine each and every tooth that formed into a spiral creeping down its throat and it only further aggravated her apprehension. She inched her way past the alarming creature and moved on in the opposite direction of where she had gone the first time around.

Glowing clouds of color completely surrounded the empress, but Renée remembered the Miracle Worker had mentioned them and she continued to advance forward while she held her breath. She may have been made of water, but inhaling the acids could prove detrimental—equivalent to a human breathing in toxic gases. At last she made it to another room in the cavern, the very last one in her search for the entrance to the Cataras Springs.

Just as Renée expected, colorful beams of light shot down from the mossy ceiling and faded away into the darkness beneath her. After mulling it over for a nervous minute, she remembered that she had been instructed to ascend the dark blue light. As a result, she emerged into the Cataras Springs.

Captain Tzatara and his company of followers were appropriately upset to hear that Rein did not have the key as they had expected.

"Who has the key?" asked Yacomé, the first mate.

"My friend traded it for a miracle from the Mystery Miracle Worker," Rein answered.

"Ye made a vow!" the captain exclaimed.

"I made a vow to let you in, not that I would have the key," Rein said.

"Well then how are ya supposed to let me in?"

"We must wait for the Mystery Miracle Worker." Rein swallowed. "You all waited a long time to find this place, you can spare more time. She said she'd be here soon."

The Mystery Miracle Worker, who was still hiding behind the tree, glimpsed at Stephocra and shrugged.

"I suppose there's no way of avoiding it, huh?" She strolled toward the pirates and pixie.

"How long exactly?" Yacomé asked.

"She just said soon," Rein answered with a shrug. "I assume sometime today."

"Ah, Jericho Tzatara," said the Miracle Worker once she was close enough to be heard. "We meet again at last."

"Ah, well if it isn't the legendary Mystery Miracle Worker," replied the captain. "Ye wouldn't happen to have the key on ya now, would ya?"

"I might," the Miracle Worker replied. "Or perhaps I'm waiting for another Mystery Miracle Worker to show up, but that doesn't seem likely, now does it?"

"Wonderful!" Rein exclaimed, clearly relieved. "Now if you don't mind, the inhabits are in the process of evacuation. They shouldn't be much longer."

"We have no interest in whatever creatures live here," said Yacomé.

"Just humor me," Rein deadpanned. "I told you they won't be much longer."

"How much longer?"

Rein rolled her eyes. "Very well, I'll go check."

Rein disappeared inside the tree that reflected everything around it, excluding the people. Captain Tzatara touched it to make sure it was solid and indeed it was.

"So, Jericho," said the Miracle Worker. "I recall I left a tiny box of clothes and accessories on your ship last time we saw each other."

"I still have it," Captain Tzatara replied. "I don't mind returning it once we're finished here."

"So what are we waiting for?" Yacomé asked. "We have the key, we don't have to wait anymore."

"Have patience, Picaroon," the Miracle Worker replied. "It's not as though the Springs will be destroyed anytime soon."

Captain Tzatara recognized the sly grin on the Mystery Miracle Worker's face to mean that the Cataras Springs were most certainly going to be destroyed soon. However, since she appeared to be unalarmed, he also remained calm.

"Well they should be gone by now. Let's go!"

"Calm down, Yacomé!" said the captain. "We will wait."

Stephocra extended his hood with a threatening hiss directed at Yacomé, who took a nervous step back from the snake. The Miracle Worker shot him an irritated glance but thought it wise to hold her tongue. At long last, Rein returned.

"Everyone's gone," she informed, and she then disappeared back into the mirror-tree.

The Mystery Miracle Worker flicked her wrist and the key appeared in her palm. She placed it into the center of the tree, turned it, and a bright silver light outlined a door complete with a platinum doorknob. The Miracle Worker twisted the knob and opened the door to reveal a limestone stairwell that descended into a glorious garden of glistening grass, vines, and flowers. The Miracle Worker was the first to enter, then Captain Tzatara, followed by Yacomé and the rest of the pirates. Once everyone was inside, the door closed and vanished so that no one else may enter.

Chapter Nineteen

The garden of the Cataras Springs was the most beautiful wonder on Xyntriav at its time. Specks of gold light floated about the brightly-colored trees and bushes. Mossy vines draped the silverstone walls and bright, colorful bubbles served themselves as rocks beside the shimmering rivers and streams. The sweet smell of lotus, lilies, lilac, and lavender was so strong that the visitors could taste it. And though the Springs were located underground, there still seemed to be a light blue moonlight present to illuminate everything in this enclosure.

"Me eyes have never beheld such a sight," murmured Captain Tzatara.

"Aye," agreed Yacomé with his jaw dropped.

There was one visible waterfall right beside the entrance which poured into the same body of water through which Empress Renée had entered. However, once the empress noticed the additional visitors, she remained hidden in the illuminated pond.

The Mystery Miracle Worker went straight to business. She approached the labradorite fountain located in what could be considered the courtyard of this garden. It displayed every chalice needed to utilize the Springs, and Rein sat silent at the top. The Miracle Worker took hold of the sky-blue chalice and gave Rein a friendly wink before she began her search for the proper spring. This was destined to be a difficult task to say the least. The more valuable the spring, the harder it was to find, although the soothing sound of the trickling waters surrounded the visitors like a tease.

"What's she doing?" Yacomé asked.

"Never mind her," the captain replied. "Let's take care of our own business."

Captain Tzatara approached the fountain next, and he snatched up the black chalice before he proceeded to seek out his desired spring. Yacomé followed with the rest of the pirate troop and Rein watched them progress deeper into the garden. Then she removed the glove on her left hand. Relief flowed through her when she noticed the mark of her oath had vanished.

Once everyone was absent from the courtyard, Empress Renée emerged and approached Rein. She kept her gray cloak tight around her to hide her missing arm and then she studied the remaining chalices.

"Which one is mine?" she asked.

"I'm not going to tell you, Renée," Rein replied.

The empress glared at her. "You might as well tell me, I'm here now!"

"No. Trust me you don't want to have anything to do with these springs."

The empress ignored her and sought after the Mystery Miracle Worker with the hope she could gather more information from her. Rein rolled her eyes.

"Renée!" she called. "Let me explain! I'll tell you everything!"

But the empress ignored her and melted into water before Rein could fly after her.

"Renée, I'll tell you why. I'll tell you everything! Renée!"

The Mystery Miracle Worker searched carefully for the spring she needed, fully aware that they were obnoxiously easy to miss. All the while she still kept an eye out for Ravan, even though the door to the garden had disappeared along with the key. Listening for the springs was the least helpful method of discovery since they sounded like they were everywhere. So, she relied on her sight and felt around for water flowing down the trees and around the rocks.

"What knowledge have you on finding the spring, Miss?" Stephocra asked her as she felt along a tree.

"Very little," the Miracle Worker admitted. She moved on and searched between a cluster of rocks. "I'm assuming they're camouflaged."

She stuck her fingers between the rocks and found the grass damp. A grin tugged at the corner of her mouth. She followed the moisture through leaves and bushes and found a tiny spring beneath a flowery shrub.

"You found it!" said Stephocra.

"Don't get too excited." The Miracle Worker dipped the chalice in the water. "That's not it."

"How can you be sure?"

"The chalice is supposed to disappear, remember?"

They continued their search.

"So which was that?" Stephocra asked.

"I don't know, perhaps one of the wonders that aren't as grand as the healing spring. It could be the beauty or the strength spring."

The empress listened in on their conversation and almost jumped for joy when she learned that the Mystery Miracle Worker was looking for the same spring she was. Renée followed her and Stephocra for the rest of their search. She remained in the form of a pool of water to keep out of sight since the Miracle Worker constantly glanced over her shoulder.

Then the Miracle Worker stopped at a particular tree where water spilled over her hand and led underground. She felt along the grass and followed the trail of moisture to an area blanketed with lavender leaves and blooming with bluebells. She felt along the ground when suddenly her hand went straight through the cover of leaves and into a pond where morning glories lined the bottom.

The Miracle Worker was confident she had found it now. She submerged the chalice into the water and watched as it vanished before her eyes. She and Stephocra smiled at the sight. The Miracle Worker brought the chalice back and examined at the water it held.

"Can you imagine, Stephocra?" she asked. "The ability to heal anything and everything immediately in one chalice. It's unfathomable."

The Miracle Worker poured the water into one of the odd-looking bottles she had brought with her and then corked it.

"There," she said. "Let's go find the captain."

The Miracle Worker left the chalice by the spring and Renée felt relief and excitement rush through her body. She had finally reached the Spring of Healing after all this time! Now, she could bear her own children and her subjects would look upon her as noble for her title! Then she would save her adopted daughter and the entire empire would declare her worthy of praise! At long last!

Renée used the chalice to drink from the spring and downed the whole cup. Moments after ingesting the spring-water, she watched as her arm slowly grew back. It was an astonishing sight and it frightened her almost as much as losing the arm had. She took a moment to repose before she summoned a bottle from the moisture in the air and collected some of the water from the spring. Then she corked the bottle and carefully made her way back to the courtyard of the garden.

The Mystery Miracle Worker and Stephocra caught up to Captain Tzatara and Yacomé to find that they had not yet found the spring they were looking for.

"Come to help us find the Spring of Agelessness?" asked Captain Tzatara.

"Actually," replied the Miracle Worker, "we were hoping that you might've found it for us."

"Aw, what a shame."

"Quite. Tell you what, you agree to let us use the chalice after you and I'll help you find it."

"Sure ye have the ability?" the captain challenged.

"I've already found the Spring of Healing."

"Did ya now?" Captain Tzatara glanced at Yacomé and his other fellow privateers. "I don't see any harm in it, so long as we get first drink."

"Deal."

They shook hands and continued their search. The Miracle Worker used her same technique, but this one proved harder to find. She found a couple of springs, but none of them were the correct one.

"I wish there be a map to this place," Yacomé said.

"You and everyone else in the world, Picaroon," said the Miracle Worker without looking at him.

The pirates copied the Miracle Worker's routine, but of course she knew her own routine best. She felt along the wet ground until the moisture stopped on top of a small hill and she concluded that there was a spring beneath where she stood. The Miracle Worker jumped down from the hill to find that it stood a little above her waist. She felt along it and after a while of seemingly getting nowhere, she found a break in the ground. It appeared that half of this hill was a large rock covered in moss and grass. With the help of the captain and some of his men, they pried the rock aside to reveal a small spring beneath it. Water trickled down from the top of the tiny hill and dribbled into a pool full of gardenias and surrounded by a multitude of lavender flowers

"Try it," the Miracle Worker said to Captain Tzatara.

He obeyed and dipped the chalice into the water. It vanished.

"This be it!" cried the captain.

The Miracle Worker smiled and patiently waited for him and his crew to drink their shares.

"Ah, it just makes ye feel so warm inside," Yacomé said after taking a drink.

"Aye, it does," the captain agreed. He finally turned to the Miracle Worker. "Ah, almost forgot about ye. A deal's a deal ain't it? Here, yer turn." He tossed her the chalice and she caught it with ease. "Think ya can tell us where the Spring of Healing be?"

"I could, but you wouldn't be able to drink from it today," said the Miracle Worker as she double-checked to make sure that this was in fact the correct spring.

"How come?" asked Yacomé.

"Because if you drink from more than one spring in the same day, you'll die. I'm surprised you didn't know that."

"Didn't you just drink from it?"

"No." The Miracle Worker showed him the bottle. "I bottled it for research."

"Thank ya for letting us know," said the captain. "Take care now."

"You too, Jericho," the Miracle Worker replied.

Once the pirates had left, the Miracle Worker drank a cupful of the ageless water and gave some to Stephocra.

"It does make you feel warm, doesn't it?" she mentioned.

"Yes, indeed," Stephocra replied.

The Miracle Worker poured some of the water into the second bottle she had brought with her.

"Well Stephocra, our work here is done. Let's go home."

When the pirates and the Mystery Miracle Worker had left the garden, Renée found that she preferred not to leave the same way she had arrived and made her way toward the door to the Cataras Springs. Rein caught sight of the empress with her blueglass bottle and opted to try to get through to her one last time.

"Renée," she called. "Put it back!"

"Rein, don't even try," said the empress without turning to look at her.

"Won't you even let me explain why we don't want you to take the water to Nadia?"

"Go home, Rein," said the empress as she exited. "You got your wings, and I'm running out of time."

Rein took the key from the threshold and tossed it into the garden before she chased after the empress.

"Renée!" she shouted. "The water doesn't work outside the garden!"

Fed up, the empress began melting into water, and at this point Rein panicked. Though she may fail in the end, she would succeed at one thing concerning this imperial family. She charged full speed at the empress and collided with the bottle, knocking it out of her hand. Both girls watched with jaws dropped as the glass shattered against a rock and the water inside disintegrated all that it touched like acid.

"What have you *done*?" Empress Renée wailed.

"I've saved your daughter," Rein spat. "You wouldn't *listen*! All this time, we've been telling you the Springs will *not* help you find joy. As you can see, this is one reason why. We've always been honest with you. You need a bottle made by elves and blessed by fairies, and you must pour the water into them using the chalice. Otherwise, the waters turn to acid when they leave the Cataras Springs."

"Then why didn't Tiana give me one of those?" Renée roared.

"For the love of all that shines, why don't you *listen*?" Rein shouted back. "You were unhappy before Nadia, this wasn't the answer!"

"Curse all of you!" the empress wailed. "This is *your* fault! Now Nadia will be enchanted and sent to land, and the fault lies with you and your noble Fairy Circle! A curse on all your kind!"

With that, Empress Renée melted to the ground and made her way back to the Obsidian Palace. Rein choked back her tears and pressed her guilt deep down in her soul. Indeed, much that had happened was her fault. Many questionable characters had accessed the Springs that day, and yes that was on her. She hadn't tried very hard to stop

Renée, and now Nadia was to be banished from her home. She was partially responsible for that as well. All she could do now was try some way to redeem herself. To start, Rein flew off to see how she could continue to help the former inhabitants of the Cataras Springs make their way to the Maja Forest.

Later, when the island had been completely evacuated, the mysterious man in the silver cloak emerged from the woods and approached the mirror-tree where his reflection failed to show. He peered around for a moment to make sure no one was present before he revealed a bejeweled dagger from beneath his cloak. Then he stepped into the very center of the empty space, raised the dagger above his head, and plunged it into the soil. A silver burst of energy expanded from the blade and the ground opened up beneath him. With the dagger still in his fist, the man tumbled into the crater that had formed and touched down on a speck of land in the middle of a pond.

Now that he had finally entered the Cataras Springs, it was time to find the chalice for his reward. Ravan sheathed the dagger and strode up to the black fountain. Clearly he knew exactly where to go and what to do; it was almost as if he had been there before.

Upon arriving at the glistening display of chalices, Ravan snatched the lavender chalice and went to find his spring of choice. This, too, took very little time at all. After some minor searching, he came upon one of several large logs. He scraped one log with his hand until he exposed a small emerald that blended in with the rest of the moss. Ravan matched it to one of the jewels on his dagger and the jewels lit up. He shoved the log aside in a struggle that was long and tedious, but he soon uncovered what lay beneath it—a spring. He dipped the chalice into the water and watched it disappear. The only part of his face that could be seen in the shadow of his hood was his impish smile.

Ravan drank a full cup of the water and felt a glorious pang shoot through his body, enclosing him in a dreadful paradise. It was agonizing, but it was holy, and it forced laughter from his lungs. Then the sensation of awful perfection slowly receded, leaving behind the assurance that he had finally achieved that which he had been searching for eons—Power!

"So," he breathed. "This is what it feels like."

Chapter Twenty

Back at the Obsidian Palace beneath the Aquamarine Ocean, Empress Renée had picked up a mussel shell and stormed into a garderobe for privacy before speaking with anyone. She required immediate answers before she could face any seafolk. There she urinated on the underside of the shell and set it aside for a minute to process. She paced dramatically in the tiny chamber, anxiously waiting for the time to pass quicker.

"Change color," she growled at the shell. "Change, *change*!"

Nothing happened to the color of the shell. Once the minute was up, the empress bashed and punched the walls of the garderobe. The Mystery Miracle Worker's theory had been proven accurate, at least in Renée's case.

"Curse you!" Renée cried. "You did this to me!"

After she had calmed down to some degree, Empress Renée explained to her husband everything that had happened during the last month and a half. Though of course, she tweaked the bit about healing her womb.

Emperor Jaskaran sat in front of the ornate lavachamber in the large drawing room listening intently, though he took everything Renée said with a grain of sea-salt. Once she had finished speaking, he took a moment to process her words and stood to face the magma of the lavachamber, which was essentially the ocean's version of a fireplace.

"So what do you plan to do now, Renée?" he asked.

"What do *I* plan to do?" Renée was disgusted. "Don't you think it's time for *you* to do something?"

"I've tried," Jaskaran replied, striving desperately not to raise his voice. He turned to face his wife, placating his hands at his side. "I've asked you on multiple occasions what I could do to help you. But I'll ask you again: What do you need from me to make you feel better?"

Empress Renée stood beside the coral settee and dug deep within her for an answer. "I don't know," she choked. "I don't know anymore. It's hopeless."

Their Majesties both stood in silence wondering, *what next?* Then Renée realized that they only had three days left before the Rose Tree finished growing branches, and the miracle worker would come looking for Nadia.

"You must help me hide Nadia." The desperation was evident in her voice.

"Renée, I want to lose her as much as you do, but I don't find it wise to go against God."

"She's our child, not His! They can't take her from us!"

"Calm down, Renée. Listen, I never said that I was going to go down without a fight at all. I will speak with the miracle worker. Perhaps we can negotiate something."

"We can have her executed for treason! That's exactly what will happen! If she refuses to work with us, you will sentence her to death, or I will kill that witch myself."

Renée refused to speak further about the matter and stormed out of the drawing room leaving Jaskaran behind, torn and at a loss.

Emperor Jaskaran did not permit his wife to be present the following day when the miracle worker arrived to meet with him. He sat with the hag-eel hybrid in the same drawing room, and together they took tea in front of the lavachamber.

"Your wife is toxic, Your Majesty," the miracle worker said bluntly. "She lack in much, including self-control and encouragement."

"I understand this, but should I suffer as well?" asked Emperor Jaskaran. "There must be some room for negotiation. Nadia's health has improved since Renée's been gone for over a month. And is the curse really necessary?"

"You talk to your wife about the curse, sire," the miracle worker answered. "However, I can offer comfort. Your child will live with the king and queen of Noelle, and when your wife is no longer around, she will be able to visit."

Emperor Jaskaran's eyes widened. "You mean upon Renée's death?"

"The child is leaving the ocean because she cannot be around your wife," the miracle worker explained. "You will surely outlive the empress, sire. You will see Nadia again, but the child need to be in an environment where she can grow wit honor, learn life lessons such as empatty and endurance, and understand the influences of love. The empress express few of these, and she will only cause Nadia's mental and physical healt to decline."

Emperor Jaskaran rubbed his face and then ran his fingers through his hair. "I want what's best for Nadia," he finally choked. "If that's what this is, then so be it."

The miracle worker nodded and set her tea down. "I will at lease provide the empress wit these final two days. Maybe she surprise us both."

Later that day, Emperor Jaskaran thought to administer to his wife a little test, mostly with the hope that it will accomplish something to the benefit of everyone. He informed Empress Renée that he had convinced the miracle worker to allow them to keep Nadia by saying Renée had found joy, but she would have to back him up and prove that this was true. At the time, Renée expressed thankfulness and agreed that she would, and she even felt that she could.

The for the rest of that day and into the night, Empress Renée felt victorious. She had convinced her husband to reason with the miracle worker, who had in turn convinced her to leave Nadia alone. The next morning, she even woke up in a contented mood. She opted to have breakfast in bed before taking a stroll through her courtyard. While this courtyard felt different after her unfortunate adventure, she couldn't say that it felt better. It was during this thought when Nadia swam out of the palace with a small coral dolphin in her hand. Renée eyed the merchild, and a feeling she hadn't experienced before claimed her heart. Or maybe this feeling hadn't been as evident before…

"Look, Mother!" she called excitedly. "I carved it myself!"

Renée took the sculpted piece from Nadia and turned it over in her hand, examining it closely. "Why are you carving coral?"

"It's part of the crafts section of my lessons, Mother," Nadia explained. "It's my favorite. Miss Octren says I have a talent!"

"Your governess is allowing this?" Renée asked displeased. "That's ridiculous, what a horrid waste of time. Take me to her at once!"

The smile vanished from Nadia's face. "I can simply tell her, Mother. We can move on to other lessons."

"Don't be silly, I will tell her myself."

Empress Renée flowed quickly to confront Nadia's octopus governess and held nothing back as she laid into Miss Octren and demanded to review the lesson plans herself. Nadia felt horrible for getting her governess in trouble with her mother and cried, apologizing profusely. She had been so proud of the carving and wanted to show it to someone, but her father had been detained. Of course, Miss Octren blamed Nadia for nothing.

Later that afternoon when Empress Renée reviewed the lesson plans with the governess, Miss Octren insisted that there should be fun and leisurely activities sprinkled between lessons, but Renée refused to listen. The purpose of an education was to teach useful lessons. Arts and crafts should be reserved for hobbies. This was the spark of the continuous descent of Renée's attitude back to the sour stage it had been only a day prior. Her bitter mood spread about the palace again with a rapid pace. Nadia, once more, failed to enjoy her mother's presence and actively avoided her as much as possible. It did not take Emperor Jaskaran the entire two remaining days to realize that the miracle worker had been correct all along, and he even started to look forward to sending Nadia away to a more promising life. If only he understood what the miracle worker meant by talking to his wife about Nadia's curse...

On the night of the final day, the miracle worker of the Aquamarine Ocean crept up to the palace with a small bag that contained something which glowed. Once she got as close to the palace as she thought she could without being seen by the guards armed with massive spears, she opened the bag to release four tiny glowfish. The guards played with them for a little while until suddenly, a glowfish shot down each of their throats, immediately rendering them unconscious. When the glowfish returned to the bag, the miracle worker swam past the sleeping guards and entered the palace. All the while, Empress Renée stood nervously at her amber chamber window listening, watching, worrying.

Emperor Jaskaran tried to sleep but he felt worried as well and could only stare at the wall with drowsy eyes.

The miracle worker let the glowfish swim down the marble corridor ahead of her to knock out whoever might be approaching while she quietly made her way to Nadia's chamber. She arrived at the princess's oyster-shell door to find that the fish had already taken out the six mermen guarding it. One glowfish unlocked the door and the miracle worker entered to see the twelve-year-old princess fast asleep in her black oyster bed. The sound of the miracle worker's entry awakened Nadia and she sat up to get a better look at the intruder. The miracle worker released a single glowfish, which shot toward Nadia who screamed. This enabled the fish to shoot down her throat and knock her out as well. Nadia's scream alerted the guards outside her own amber window. Unfortunately, they were also no match for the miracle worker's tactics and hardly made it into the chamber before they were put to sleep.

Empress Renée and Emperor Jaskaran heard Nadia's scream as well and they quickly made their way to their daughter's chamber, only to find the bedroom window open, the guards floating about out cold, and Nadia missing. Empress Renée went ballistic and as much as Emperor Jaskaran was distraught about the situation, Renée's constant meltdowns were becoming more of a nuisance than he could stand.

"She's gone!" Renée wailed. "Oh my god, she's gone!"

"Renée, please," said Jaskaran.

This set the empress off to levels never seen before. Always being dismissed. Always second place. She turned red and quaked with her fists clenched before she erupted like a hurricane with overwhelming powerful emotion. "Curse you! Curse you and your children! You're weak, and may whatever strength you have left leave you as well!"

Realization overcame Jaskaran and in a desperate attempt to stop her, he brought his hand down on Renée. "*Silence*!" he bellowed. "My god, what have you done? Are you blind to your own actions?"

Renée gaped blankly at Jaskaran. She had never seen her husband like this and was lost in how to react. She watched him as he pushed his hair back with both hands and faced the guards.

"Lock her in separate chambers!"

"What?" Renée cried as she was led away against lava-tipped staffs. "Oh my god, you let the miracle worker in! You showed her to Nadia's chamber! How dare you put the blame on me! How can you live with yourself? Curse you as well with your weak heart! You're powerless to your simplest enemies!"

Emperor Jaskaran watched his raving wife disappear down another corridor and one of his imperial advisors approached him when all was silent.

"Would you like to send out a search party for the princess, sire?" he asked.

"No," said the emperor with a heavy sigh. "Maybe the miracle worker is right and this is the best thing for her. I don't wish for my daughter to be anywhere around the empress, especially after that display. Tomorrow, bring me the Chevess of Ocean Rose. I wish to assign her with a task."

With that, Emperor Jaskaran left to mourn and pray in his chambers.

During this time in the Maja Forest, Queen Tiana met with the other twelve fairies of the Fairy Circle, where they discussed a most important topic.

"I can't believe this has happened," said a fairy by the name of Luella. "And so soon!" She dressed in black and red and bore the power to foresee the death of anything.

"It's been about four centuries," another fairy named Larien replied. He dressed in black and orange and bore the power to increase bodily strength. "What I would like to review is why we created the Cataras Springs in the first place"

"I remember it being because we wanted to create something interesting for all who live on Xyntriav," answered Queen Tiana. "To give them something to do, something to keep them busy. To give them hope. And also a place for the merpixies to live."

"The merpixies are perfectly capable of living here like the rest of us," claimed a fairy dressed black and green. This was Narissa. She had the power to manipulate spring and plant-life.

"Yes, but you know how shy and unsociable they are," added a blue and black fairy named Avery. He had the power to manipulate winter and weather.

"Well the Springs have only created problems," mentioned a purple and black fairy. This was Aranel who was able to see the present virtually anywhere in the world. "Do you realize how dangerous this situation was? Not only has someone had access to those wonders, but a *pirate* had access to it."

"*Many* pirates," added Faye, a fairy dressed in autumn colors. She had the ability to manipulate emotions and autumn. "And these weren't even the first pirates to have access to them!"

"That's correct!" commented Elwyn, who was dressed in black and gold. "We're lucky they only drank from the ageless spring!" This fairy bore the power to increase the purpose of an object. For instance, he could make a single sip of ale cause one to be stumbling drunk for an entire day if he wished it.

"I concur," said Queen Tiana. "And this is why we're going to destroy the Springs. And I'm sure we all agree on this, so why are we still discussing it?"

"Because *I* think it wise to destroy every wonder we have created along with the Cataras Springs," announced Ailsa, a black and white fairy with the power to summon and repel.

"Now let's not be ridiculous, Ailsa," Queen Tiana replied. "There's no need to be so extreme with this incident. Not all of our wonders are so dangerous."

"I'm sure we can name a few," said a fairy dressed in cool colors. "After all, how many wonders have we created?" This fairy, Alverdine, had the ability to heal and protect.

"Thirteen, not including the Cataras Springs," said the queen. "And I'm sure I can name more helpful wonders than dangerous ones."

"Please, name them," said Frieda, a fairy dressed in black and pink with the power to increase beauty.

"There's the zoilie stone, the Darigo Mountains—"

"The Darigo Mountains can be a problem," interrupted the warm-colored fairy named Alvara. She bore the power to manipulate summer and the elements.

"We can't destroy a mountain range!"

"We can make it so that it's not dangerous!" Sebille insisted. She was dressed in black and yellow and had the ability to make things age in reverse.

"So, you want us to kill every dragon in existence?" Avery asked.

"Why not? What good are they to us?"

"They do a lot of good!"

"All right, how about this," Queen Tiana offered. "Since the Springs are the more important issue at hand, let's take care of it and destroy them. *Then* we may discuss the other wonders we have created. As I'm sure Aranel can verify, they are not a current problem. Agreed?"

Aranel nodded her head and everyone concurred. The meeting ended.

Rein watched the Fairy Circle destroy the Cataras Springs while she was still on the island. The Mystery Miracle

Worker and Stephocra watched the scene from atop the cave they lived in while snacking on strips of jerky. The many rays of color and light lit up the sky like foreign fireworks and it was arguably the most awe-inspiring sight all three of them had ever seen or ever will see.

Once the Cataras Springs had been destroyed, Rein made her way back to the continent of Noelle to make sure the former inhabitants of the Springs had made it back safely. Once she confirmed they had, she left the Maja Forest and made it her personal job to look after Princess Nadia. She would redeem herself for her reckless behavior during the past two months.

During this time, the miracle worker of the Aquamarine Ocean put a recipe together in a large seashell she set on a marble podium. She plucked a strand of crimson hair from the unconscious princess's head and let it sink onto the concoction, then watched it burn and explode into a purple cloud. Then the mixture crystallized into tiny, purple, star-like pieces and she poured them into a small sack. She packed it along with some clothes for Nadia to wear on land and the golden ball that she had mentioned to Empress Renée in the beginning.

On a beach outside of Helvetica, the miracle worker lay Princess Nadia in a cave and set the clothes aside. She then brought out the bag of purple crystals and set it beside Nadia. While she waited for the princess to awaken, the miracle worker started a fire and dried the clothes Nadia was to wear. Eventually, the princess woke up and glanced around the cave with a dumbfounded expression on her face.

"Oh good, you're awake," the miracle worker said.

Nadia gaped at the hag in terror, astonished by her hideous appearance. The miracle worker ignored her and continued speaking.

"Eat the crystals in the bag."

Nadia eyed the bag next to her and opened it. She was unsure about eating it and wondered if she should trust her kidnapper.

"Well go on," the miracle worker insisted.

The hag frightened the princess, so she obeyed. After Nadia had finished the last crystal, she watched in horror as her fishtail slowly separated and morphed into two legs. The transformation appeared painful and it was terrifying to watch, but she felt hardly anything.

"What have you done?" Nadia cried once the transformation was complete.

"You can't live in the ocean anymore. You live on land now. Put these on. Get some rest." The miracle worker threw the dried clothes at Nadia. "Tomorrow morning, you go to the palace on the cliff." She pointed behind Nadia. "Their Majesties are especting you. Tell them you parents died and told you to come to the palace, you don't know why. Avoid people on your way dare. You age slower than landfolk, so tell everyone you are ten years old. If anyone asks, your name is Sierna and you're running an errand for your family, then walk away. Answer no more questions and don't let anyone know you're mermaid. You're allowed to take your mermaid form for no more than tree days at a time by submerging yourself for a minute. You die if you stay a mermaid longer. Then wait two weeks before you take on the form again. Dis way you can return to get more of these crystals. You need to eat another bag every tree years.

"Another very important ting. Your mutter has cursed you. Dis golden ball is your life. If someone touches it, you lose your strength and grow weak. You have a month to touch the ball again before you die. *Keep it hidden* at all times. No one can know it exists. *No one.* Do you understand everyting I say?"

Nadia, who was now dressed, nodded her head even though she only remembered half of what the miracle worker had told her.

"Good," said the miracle worker. "Practice walking. It be difficult, but you must master it before you go to the palace. Good luck, Princess."

Without another word, the miracle worker left Nadia there in the dark, empty cave and returned to the ocean. Nadia's eyes bounced about the rocky structure around her, and then down at her two, strange new limbs. She eyed the fire in front of her and reached out toward the odd dancing light. Her hand suddenly recoiled at the extreme heat and she hugged her trembling body. She didn't understand any of this, and she knew very little of the world above the ocean. She was only aware of what Miss Octren had taught her, the pictures she saw in her lesson books, and the stories she read on her own. Soon it occurred to Nadia that she was officially alone in an extraordinary world to which she was ignorant, and she felt a sob forming in her throat.

At this time, Rein patrolled the coast of Helvetica after hearing rumors about the location to which Princess Nadia was being taken, and she spotted a faint glow emanating from one of the caves which lined the beach. Her heart skipped in excitement and she dove down to peer into the cave.

"Nadia?" Rein asked.

Nadia's eyes widened at the sight of the pixie. "You know me?" she asked with a trembling voice.

"I'm a friend of family," Rein said softly. "My name is Rein Bow. Two words."

"I don't understand," Nadia choked. "What's happening?"

"Your mother is a danger to you, so it was thought that the land might provide you with a better opportunity for a more prosperous life. You'll grow comfortable quickly and you'll like the Helvetican Palace better than your last home. You'll also be able to visit your father every once in a while. So you'll be fine, all right? I'm going to help you out as much as I can."

Nadia nodded her head. She felt a smidgen of relief to have someone who would help her. She pointed at the fire.

"What's that?" she asked.

"That's fire," Rein answered. "From what I hear, you use lava in the same way we use fire up here."

"Oh, I've read about fire," said Nadia. "You have fireplaces and we have lavachambers."

Rein perched on a rock beside the princess. "Oh, that's interesting. Have you had a chance to try out your new legs?"

Nadia glanced down at them again and shook her head. "No, they feel funny."

Rein scratched her head. "I imagine they would. Well, I suppose get used to them for a little, but you should definitely practice on them before you enter Helvetica."

"What's that?" Nadia asked.

"That's the town the palace is located in."

Nadia and Rein sat in the cave and talked around the fire for a short time. Rein tried to focus on the more shocking aspects the princess may encounter the following day, and then coached her when she tried using her legs. Eventually, it was time to get some sleep and Rein watched over the princess for a while before she decided she should rest too. Nadia would soon learn that everything was going to be just fine. Rein would make sure of that.

Epilogue

During the past three hundred fifty years, since Gerardo of Liko was last heard of, the Kingdom of Noelle had thrived and gone through a number of extreme changes; some of which included art, food, morale, literature, currency (so that it was less confusing), and especially law. The country now had become very wealthy with markets in gold, silk, and cotton. The fashion was more colorful and the architecture was shapelier with geometric and floral designs. But after roughly three hundred years, an end was arising to this period and a medieval era was slowly underway.

The towns were now built of wood and adobe, with streets of stone and had increased in size and population. Aqueducts ran through each one, so drought was now rare. And as one can expect technology to develop in a different order and speed on a different world, it is understandable how plumbing was invented immediately following the aqueduct. Unfortunately, the plumbing lines were only in the process of being built, so there were still wells in every town and in the backyards of the especially wealthy.

The palace of the Kingdom of Noelle was gorgeous, especially in the sunny weather the Noellites had on Malla 35, 836 (April 17). The sunlight reflected off the dome towers and the sea breeze blew through the windows into the king and queen's bedchamber. The queen stirred under her satin bed sheets before she finally opened her violet eyes. It was clear by the look on her tanned face that she was disturbed. She glanced over at her husband who was still asleep and she decided not to wake him. Instead, she carefully got out of bed and wrapped herself in a white, silk robe. Then she sat at her silver vanity and brushed her bright pink locks as she watched herself in the mirror. If only she could get that disturbing dream out of her mind.

"Up so early, Ariana?" asked the king.

Queen Ariana jumped at the sudden sound of her husband's voice. "You startled me, Darren," she said with a smile.

"I'm sorry, Dear," replied King Darren. "How did you sleep?"

"Fair, I suppose. Yourself?" Ariana went back to messing with her hair.

"I slept wonderfully." Darren got out of bed and stretched his bulky body. "And I had the most fantastic dream. So realistic and so beautiful."

"Really?" Ariana asked, interested. "What was it about?"

"Well, the setting was today and we were both in the throne room. Suddenly, the guards escorted in this man with an adorable little girl of about ten years old. The man told us that he bought her from the market and that he thought we'd like to have her work for us, and oh—I could see her so clearly!"

The smile on the queen's face slowly vanished as the king continued to explain his dream to her.

"She had beautiful crimson hair, bright blue eyes, and glowing skin as white as a pearl. And her lips were so luscious and bright red. Such a lovely child. She said her name was—"

"Nadia," the queen finished for him. There was a look of concern on her face. "She said her parents had died and we agreed to let her stay with us. In the end, she married the heir to the throne."

King Darren looked at her in astonishment. "How did you know?"

"I had the same dream. So vivid, I remember everything."

There was a moment of silence before the king asked, "Do you think there's something more to this dream?"

Ariana hoped not. "I'm not sure."

That afternoon, King Darren and Queen Ariana were in a drawing room consulting with their royal advisor about their dream. The queen paced around in a state of anxiety and the king remained seated on the sofa, leaning forward in anticipation.

"Well, from what I hear, this is a very special dream," said the advisor.

"Clearly, Polaris," said Darren. "But can you tell us why we both had this same dream?"

"I can," Polaris replied as he stood up and walked around. He dressed in a gold shirt with large sleeves and a black vest. "There have been many studies on these kinds of occurrences, all leading to the same conclusion. These dreams are meant to happen, eventually. If there's a particular time set in the dream, it's said to happen at that exact time."

"Oh, this is wonderful!" exclaimed the king. "Ariana, did you hear?" The queen did her best to express equal excitement. "This child, this Nadia, is coming to live with us and marry Myrdor! Oh, our son is going to have the most divine queen!"

King Darren danced out of the room and Polaris enjoyed watching the spectacle. He then looked to Queen Ariana, who did not share her husband's enthusiasm.

"Is something wrong, Your Majesty?" Polaris asked her.

She glanced at him, then looked at the floor. "Oh, nothing. I suppose I'm just confused."

Polaris smiled. "That's understandable. You'll adjust in time."

Queen Ariana nodded. "Of course."

Then she, too, left the room. Ariana went to her chamber and paced the carpeted floor, filled with angst. How could this happen? A little slave girl was going to *live* in her palace, and later even marry her eldest son. On top of that, her husband was excited about it! Such a concept was a disgrace and it was her responsibility as queen and mother to keep this dishonor from falling upon her family. But what could she do? Suddenly, she had a thought and threw herself at her desk to scribble a short letter. She sealed the envelope and summoned her lady in waiting.

"Your Majesty," said the lady in waiting with a curtsy.

"Lusi, take this letter to Count Rallian immediately. Do not return without his response. Understand? No exceptions."

"Yes, Your Majesty." Lusi curtsied and left right away.

On a hilltop just outside of Helvetica (the city of the palace) was another, smaller castle of white and gray, seemingly in constant flurry. Lusi took a coach there and looked in awe upon the estate. It had been a while since she last visited and it looked much bigger now. Just inside the large, curly, silver gate was a grand courtyard, live with exotic vegetation. It was about a three-minute ride from the gate to the front door, but it was an inspiring one as she studied the wide variety of plant-life and artwork which embellished the courtyard. Even though the estate appeared to be under some sort of construction, it was still an absolutely breathtaking sight.

Lusi left the coach for the count's servants to take care of and with her bodyguards right behind her, she lifted the skirt of her royal blue sari and climbed up the marble steps leading to the broad, iron double doors. She used the massive knocker twice and a satyr butler answered in a very timely manner.

"What can I do for you, Madam?" he asked with a face empty of emotion.

"I have a message from Her Majesty to the count," Lusi replied. "She expects a response back immediately."

"Please, come in."

The satyr led her and her bodyguards to a drawing room a few feet away from the entrance. Their shoes made such a racket on the tiled floors that Lusi was almost embarrassed and fought to make her steps lighter. She was relieved to finally make it to the drawing room where there was a rug to cover most of the area.

The satyr butler motioned them to take a seat. "Please make yourselves comfortable. His Lordship will be right with you."

"Thank you," Lusi replied.

The butler left her to study the castle with its marble pillars and silver designs painted on every inch of the building. In the room she sat, she noticed the abundance of color on the furniture and fabric as well as the gold fringe on the pillows, blankets and curtains. Even the royal palace wasn't so overly decorated.

Lusi then brought her attention to the servants and slaves, who surrounded her, and she was able to tell the two apart. The slaves were more sorrow-laden and wore gold cuffs on their right biceps. She took a moment to thank God that she was not one of them.

Finally, the count entered with a young slave girl at his right and the butler at his left. He was a large man, colorfully dressed, and he had a face that was stern but could look rather jolly when he was in the right mood.

"Can I help you?" he asked.

Lusi stood up and curtsied. "You have a letter from Her Royal Majesty, my Lord." She handed the count the letter. "She expects an immediate response."

"Sounds urgent," the count said as he opened the envelope. "Garnet, bring my writing tray."

"Yes, Master," the slave replied with a curtsy.

The count took a seat and read the letter to himself:

My Dear Friend,

I have need for your assistance, and it might very well benefit you greatly, depending on how you take advantage of my situation. There is a small girl about to be sold as a slave to a man who intends to bring her to my palace. Her name is Nadia. She is ten years of age, has crimson hair, pearl skin, bright red lips and blue eyes. I want you to see to it that she does not arrive here. I do not care how you do it. Kill her and the buyer, kidnap her from him and send her away, buy her yourself, do it however you will but I never wish to see her. This is not the end to my request but I shall explain more about this to you over tea. Come before noon.

Your Royal Queen,
Ariana of Noelle

Garnet returned with what the count had asked for and he wrote a quick response, simply saying that he was on his way over and he would give her his answer over tea. Then everyone stood up when he did and he handed his reply to Lusi.

"Thank you for your service, Madam," he said.

Lusi nodded her head. "Good day to you, sir."

Then she and her bodyguards left the castle and returned to the palace.

"Makiar," said the count to his butler.

"Yes, my Lord," Makiar replied.

"Get two men to accompany you into town. Have them read this description and see to it that you buy this girl from the slave market. Even if you have to spend a million crescents on her. Do you understand?"

"Yes, my Lord."

"Good. I have an appointment with the queen that I must attend. Send me word when you have her. I'm leaving as soon as possible with Garnet and Mauro. Have them ready in ten minutes and get the coach out front immediately. You may leave after I do."

At the palace, Queen Ariana and Count Rallian laughed and sipped tea on the balcony of a grand sitting room located on the third floor. Garnet and Mauro stood at the entrance to the balcony, dressed to the nines. They kept their faces covered and their backs turned to the two old friends, as the queen hated slaves to her core.

"Ah, Rallian," the queen said after laughing at a previous tale. "It's too bad you don't come over more often. I certainly miss your presence here."

"Yes well, I've been quite busy since I became a count," Rallian replied.

"It's a shame you had to retire. You were my best White Knight and there hasn't been one like you since."

"You flatter me, Your Majesty."

"It's true though. I'm very disappointed with my current knights. You should train them for me."

"You already have someone training them, don't you? Polaris trained me. Did you replace him?"

"No, but he says so himself that these men are a joke. I was hoping you might have a different strategy. After all, your slaves and servants seem to be well disciplined; you could probably do the same with my knights."

Rallian chuckled but he wasn't enjoying the topic of conversation. "Is this what you wanted to talk with me about?"

"No, we just came to a wrong subject," the queen answered. "What I wanted to discuss with you is the reason I need you to keep that girl from my palace, or rather, one of the reasons. It was too much to write, especially in the amount of time I had. I also didn't want to run the risk of anyone reading it."

"Well I'm all ears," said Rallian.

"I want you to pretend that you're King Klaris of Saíd, and write a letter to my husband. Here's what you're to write." Queen Ariana handed Rallian a piece of paper that had been folded many times. "An example of the seal of Saíd is in there. Have it forged and seal the letter with it."

Rallian looked at the seal and read the note. "I see. You're planning a war."

The queen smiled. "I told you I'd bring empires back into fashion someday."

"Is the king involved?"

"Oh please. He's busy adorning the palace right now in preparation for Nadia's arrival."

"Nadia?"

"She's the girl I told you to be rid of. How's that coming along, by the way?"

"I have three men on it right now. They're going to alert me when they've caught her."

"Good. So will you do this for me?"

Rallian shrugged. "Why not?" The queen smiled. "However, I want your word that my estate will not be affected by your acts of mischief. I have a lot of construction taking place and no time or money to waste."

"Very well. If anything happens to your property, I shall replace it myself with twice as much. Agreed?"

"I want that in writing."

The queen was offended that her word wasn't enough. But as long as it would get him to write that letter, she wasn't about to argue. She got up and exited the balcony. "*Move*," she snapped at Garnet and Mauro. They both stepped aside and let the queen pass. Rallian followed and watched Ariana write the contract at the desk in the sitting room. After she signed it, she handed it to him and he read it over.

"Wonderful." He placed the note in an inside coat pocket. "I shall keep this with me for future reference."

The door to the sitting room opened and they both turned their heads to see a werecat servant enter. She curtsied when she said, "Your Majesty. A message came for His Lordship."

"Bring it here," Ariana replied.

Rallian took the note and read it. He showed it to the queen and they both smiled at its contents: *We have her, sir.*

To be continued...

Have you read the entire Rose Tree Chronicles?

Printed in the USA
CPSIA information can be obtained
at www.ICGtesting.com
LVHW020000181024
794153LV00032B/789